Satisfaction

Also by Alina Reyes:

The Butcher and Other Erotica

Behind Closed Doors

Satisfaction

AN EROTIC NOVEL

Alina Reyes

TRANSLATED FROM THE FRENCH BY
DAVID WATSON

GROVE PRESS
New York

Copyright © 2002 by Editions Robert Laffont, S.A., Paris
Translation copyright © 2004 by David Watson

Published simultaneously in Canada
Printed in the United States of America

FIRST EDITION

Library of Congress Cataloging-in-Publication Data

Reyes, Alina.
  [Satisfaction. English]
  Satisfaction: an erotic novel / Alina Reyes ; translated from the French by
    David Watson.
      p. cm.
    ISBN 0-8021-4146-3
    I. Watson, David, 1959-   II. Title.
  PQ2678.E8896S2813 2004
  843'.914—dc22

                                                            2003068564

Grove Press
841 Broadway
New York, NY 10003

04 05 06 07 08   10 9 8 7 6 5 4 3 2 1

Satisfaction

α

t is in her mouth. Enormous, hard, good. Right into the back of her throat. Her cheeks, her palate, her tongue, her lips. It is fat and heavy. Hard, good. Rubbing, touching, prodding, it fills her. It fills her, it goes down to her stomach, overflows. It runs into the joints of her body.

Afterward, she is in seventh heaven. Once freed, her mouth breaks into a grin. Her eyes glaze over, she is out of this world, absorbed in her own satisfaction.

The breast, the teat, the cream, mother's milk.

Babe turns over in bed, again and again, without opening her eyes. And each time she leaves a door swinging open inside her through which her well-being slips out and anxiety seeps in. She is groaning, panting, her closed-up face is drawn with anxiety.

A warm, milky death is spurting out of the dark; the sticky sheets turn cold around her body like a corset of stone.

It wants to kill me, Babe thinks. It's after my skin. The thing sticks to her skin, that snake, that cold, slimy snake that slides up from the bottom of the bed, wraps itself around her, encloses her, presses her thighs together, dislocates her vertebrae.

Then at full speed a Southern Pacific train comes hurtling in through the window, throbbing, whistling, slicing through the night like a noisy asteroid.

O God, You who know what we have done, Bobby and I, within this bed, and what our parents did before us, and their parents before them, the immemorial crime, the seed of Evil planted in the bodies of man and woman! Spare me, O Lord, perforate me with your forgiveness!

*A*round the bed the deep, sparkling night pinned her with its staring owl eyes. She lay paralyzed, listening to the noisy silence of the shadows, their endless, amplified creaks and sighs, but in which she could no longer hear the dreary hooting that she thought had woken her from that cataleptic sleep in which, for years now, she had buried a good third of her life.

Death had entered the house. She was sure of it. Images of knives, axes, saws and huge guns sent terrible, exquisite twinges stabbing through her mind and her chest.

*N*o time to breathe. The pages of the bed are sharp, closed. She is trapped in the middle of a book, one of those books with a cover in the shape of a tombstone, filled with large, scary gilded letters, one of those old stories where the corpse comes back to life beneath six feet of freshly dug earth. In the depths of terror, the corpse taps its fingers against the lid of its black, black coffin . . . And the cemetery, the macabre cemetery with its thousands of tombstones, lined up like an army in the moonlight, the dead souls, the earthworms, the decomposing flesh, the grinning skulls, all completely silent. No one can hear Babe, when she tries to tell the world there's been a mistake, I WASN'T DEAD! Too late . . . Years later, grave robbers will open the fatal casket and find her frozen fingers gripping the side and, though there is not much left on the bones, her face twisted in sheer horror . . .

Babe opened her eyes with a start, and lay there stiff and straight, eyes and ears on alert. An old record. This sudden awakening, this black, impenetrable night, this panic: the record of her life.

Her lips opened in an O—small at first, but then wider— but her "O God" stuck in her throat, didn't even produce a murmur.

A nightmare? She tried to activate her memory, but she could scarcely remember who she was or where she was. Her limbs felt like lead due to the sleeping pills. It wasn't until a vague but nonetheless even greater anxiety took hold of her that she could make the effort to sit up and feel around in the dark for the switch of the bedside lamp.

The thin strap of her mauve satin nightie had slid down her dimpled arm, and a moon-white breast had slipped out. Her flesh gave off a smell that was both bitter and sweet; it made her want to massage it, eat it. Next to her, the pale pink pillow, color-coordinated with the comforter, bore the imprint of Bobby's head. He wasn't there.

Babe laid her hand on her heart, which was pounding away inside her rib cage like that of an animal caught in a trap. She realized her breast was exposed and readjusted her nightie slowly, casting her eye round the room to flush out any intruder who might be watching her. A face pocked with holes stared at her with a surprised look from the mirror of the dark closet. And this creature, immersed in the dim light, looked more like the ghost of a supernatural child than a grown woman.

She gathered her courage, and opened her mouth again to call for her husband. A moaning sound from the depths of the house stopped her in her tracks.

A voice, a sort of sad but obscene song, was coming up from the cellar.

She felt as if she had been whipped by a silken lash. She was now completely awake. Her hair—and her nipples—stood on end. She arched her back.

It was a long moan, long like the noise of a cat in heat, and dismal like the howl of a pack of ghosts. She waited to hear what would happen next, tingling with electricity.

She didn't move for several minutes, stared at the closed door. If Bobby had gotten up to go to the bathroom or the kitchen, why hadn't he left it open?

The house remained stubbornly silent. Babe threw back the covers and went out in her bare feet. When she opened the door of the bathroom next to the bedroom, the pale light from the window fell on the landing.

Babe glanced round the room. It was ghostly. Cold gleams reflected off its ceramic fittings, its faucets and its mirrors in all directions. It looked more like an operating theater, or even a torture chamber. She wouldn't have been surprised to find Bobby's body lying there on the tiled floor, lifeless, contused,

4

bloody. Disemboweled, hacked into pieces, decapitated, castrated, lying in a dark pool of coagulating fluid.

She stayed there a moment, captivated by this vision. A cold sweat trickled slowly down between her breasts and from the inside of her thighs down to her knees, which began to tremble. On the floor next to the tub, a round puddle gleamed like a silver dish. Babe approached slowly and recognized the magnifying mirror that she used to apply her makeup. The metal-framed glass had rolled there of its own accord, just to incite her to do what she was about to do.

She crouched down over it, legs apart, and tucked the hem of her nightie up in her neckline so that she could get a proper view of her crotch. In the magnifying mirror her open sex looked like a split tomato, or some large, blind mollusk. The cold air from the surface of the glass caressed the delicate skin. The red flesh glistened in the mirror; it seemed to ripple. The hairs licked round it like flames. The smell rose, as tangible and powerful as squids' tentacles. Babe opened her mouth, and breathed in the intoxicating language of her intimacy. From the depths of her being her body spoke. Called out.

The flesh became more and more moist, shiny like the devil himself. Babe knew he could get out through that doorway, but she didn't want to see him, so she closed her legs and stood up abruptly. She left the room and started to feel her way along the wall of the landing, her breathing shallow.

There was a faint glimmer of light on the top steps of the staircase, but then it tumbled away into a well of darkness. She started to descend, one hand on the banister, her body tensed. Every time she made the stairs creak, she stopped and lifted the hem of her nightie from her dark belly to wipe her brow.

When she reached the ground floor, Babe found no sign of Bobby, dead or alive, in either the living room or the kitchen. Now in even deeper darkness, she placed her foot on the flight of stairs that led down to the cellar.

At the first landing, the stairs made a right angle. From here Babe could see a line of light beneath the door. She could also hear muffled sounds, sporadic, incomprehensible snatches of words, like someone talking in his sleep.

Babe was gripped by a desire to know what was going on. It made her forget her fear. She resisted the temptation to go place her ear against the door. She had a better idea. She was suddenly feverish, almost delirious. The curiosity excited her, filled her with something more burning than sexual desire. She hadn't felt like this for ages; she was thrillingly alive, ready for anything.

She dashed back up the stairs and, overcoming her fears, went outside the house, just in time to see the chalky, almost full moon disappear behind an enormous cloud as compact as a mountain. The garden was now pitch-black. She went out into it; her body lost all solidity and merged into the dark mass of the night, a fortress whose labyrinthine architecture reformed with every step she took. She felt her way around the walls, quickly, silently. She found her way to the back of the house, where a spot of light could be seen through the bushes.

On all fours, Babe approached the skylight. The damp air and her own sweat stuck the satin to her white, warm, throbbing flesh, endowed with an animal life of its own, uncontrollable and triumphant. Her behind was exposed to the breeze, and the cool air felt like a blessing. A strong odor of earth and mud rose to her nostrils. Her peroxide hair tumbled down in front of her eyes. She brushed it aside and smeared her cheeks with her muddy fingers. She had a desire to eat the damp grass that smelled so sweet just inches from her face, even the earth itself. The earth was rich with all the dead it had absorbed. It was good, soothing. What body wouldn't want to enter it, or take it into itself?

Normally, Babe would have rushed off to have a wash, but now she couldn't be in her right mind, for instead of this healthy reflex she had only strange ideas in her head; they filled her with an exaggerated sense of well-being so strong it almost hurt.

Very slowly she inched forward until she could see through the grille into the cellar. The window was recessed into the wall and was covered in dirt. But she could immediately make out Bobby. The world turned on its head, and she had a dizzying view of Bobby fucking, and of herself, of herself spying on Bobby, sparkling with curiosity, herself concentrated, miniaturized by curiosity like a speck of stellar dust blasted at high speed across space by a monstrous, cosmic desire, dust to dust. She had this gripping, dizzying view of something she should have seen a long time ago.

β

Ah, les femmes . . . !" my father always used to say. These were the only words of French he brought back from the Normandy landings. That's why I thought for ages that the Second World War had been one enormous battle to conquer some vague notion of Womanhood. Ideal woman? Little women? A man must devote himself to desiring them all, and only the man who has *the power* can possess them all.

Obviously I didn't think about it precisely in those terms; I've never been that hot in the brains department. But all the same I have my own way of seeing things. For example, if I made a film about the war, I'd show that millions of soldiers were sacrificed like . . . sperm on their way to the egg. An egg called Vital Space, or Peace . . .

Yes, that's it, it's a sort of spell. Men battling for some glittering future . . . A fat mother . . . A giant . . . Ravenous

. . . Orgasmic . . . Just think what they could do with special effects. I should have been a filmmaker—no one in Hollywood has ideas like mine. People in movies spend all their time killing one another. Obviously that gets you involved. But if I made films I'd introduce some poetry into the violence . . . For example, instead of an ordinary car chase, I'd have mine in the teeth of a hurricane, with all sorts of obstacles along the way: people, animals, trees, roofs etc. smashing into the windshield . . . A family killed by the mob? OK, but I say let's have twins feeding at their mother's breasts, and let's see milk flowing with the blood . . . Whatever, this is just off the top of my head, I'm just trying to show that I'm not short on ideas. The real problem is that I just wouldn't like the Hollywood lifestyle. It's all sex, drugs, partying. I'm just a simple guy. If I got into that I'd end up sucked in, not knowing how to get out. Pity. I'd have knocked them dead with my ideas.

Anyway, during the war, the real one, like in the movies, American men, among them Johnny Wesson, the future father of Bobby, who'll never be half the man Johnny was, arrived like superheroes by air and sea and fed those half-ass Europeans a good slice of humble pie. My father never tired of telling us how the women they liberated threw themselves at their feet by the millions (or at their balls, as he put it once the empty beer cans started to pile up on and under the kitchen table where he and his pals would sit rehashing the same old stories of boozing and women year after year).

Those European women fell for the American men big-time; they just loved their broad shoulders, their chewing gum, their sense of humor and their music. From then on, their own men, shamed and confused, like the rest of the world, had no choice but to settle for second place. That's how we be-came the masters of the planet.

Ah, les femmes . . . ! Pa thought that all you had to do was keep them under your thumb, and he thought he managed that quite well. Maybe, but as he himself acknowledged out loud several times a day, that didn't mean he could understand them. *I don't understand you, Mary . . . I'll never understand women. What the fuck is going on in your head?* Etc., etc.

One night, Mom left the house while everyone was asleep. Pa must have been out of it, because he didn't even hear her start-ing the old family Plymouth. My brother and I didn't hear any-thing either. Or maybe I did wake up, but I didn't say anything, didn't move. Your memory can play tricks on you, so we'll never know for sure, not you, not me.

Mom drove all night. She parked on Daytona Beach, the only beach in the world where everyone drives, and then con-tinued on foot, leaving the key in the ignition. It was the only car we had. Then someone stole it.

She left her shoes on the sand, a pair of white pumps with short heels, like they made in those days, the late sixties. She headed straight for the sea in her sky-blue dress. She didn't stop when she reached the water. She couldn't swim; she knew what she was doing. She was the only mother we had. The sea could not refuse her.

So that's how we lost everything all at once. As Mom al-ways used to say, "Troubles never come singly." If she'd wanted to take revenge on Pa, she couldn't have done any better than deprive him of his car and his wife at the same time.

If she'd wanted to take revenge on Bobby and Timmy, who were always squabbling and giving her headaches (the consequences of which would be inflicted on Pa later in the evening), she couldn't have done any better than deprive them of a mother and abandon them to their father.

But if she'd wanted to take revenge on herself, she could have done better than take her own life: she could have stayed with her husband.

It was my eighth birthday. I didn't get a party, because Mom wasn't there to bake a cake and all the rest. Pa was mad—he was rapping his fingers, walking round in circles, holding his head in his hands to prevent his skull from exploding. He gave full vent to his annoyance, saying things like: "I can't believe the slut has walked out on me!" and: "How am I going to get to work without the car?"

Timmy was sobbing—he was four years old, he still acted like a baby with her (always in her skirts, while I just wanted to kill him).

It's like I grew up all at once. I took care of my brother: we dressed ourselves, I made breakfast, and before going to school I dropped him off with the woman next door, who would have liked to keep him.

After that we never cried, Timmy and me. Even when we learned six days later that Mom had been found on a beach, green all over, completely naked, half eaten by crabs. And they never found the car. (Or else we cried a lot as we clung to Pa, himself shattered by the shock, and later as we clung together in my bed. I can remember violent, dramatic tears, but there's no way of knowing whether I imagined them or actually experienced them.)

I know, that explains a lot. Otherwise I wouldn't be talking about it. I'm not one to dwell on the past, but it's well known that everyone needs to take stock at certain moments in their life, and this is such a moment for me. This is the first time I've tried to piece together the puzzle of my life; there aren't many pieces, it shouldn't take too long. I know Babe wouldn't agree with that. She reads women's magazines with all those personality tests, and she thinks we're all extremely complicated, especially me (everyone thinks I'm complicated and mysterious, but the only mysterious thing about me is that I'm very simple—they're all very simple, like a child's puzzle, but they don't want to admit it).

After the death of my mother, I went from being a borderline dunce to a borderline good but virtually autistic pupil (I thought of myself as an adult by now). A little later I started growing hair in places there wasn't any before, and I discovered a new source of consolation: my dick.

No need to spell it out, everyone knows the score. Serial masturbation, teenage rebellion, fights with my father, first girlfriends, drinking, wishing I were dead . . . Whatever the variations, you can't avoid it: you have to go through the hell of adolescence. You emerge from it bolted up securely like a rancid cunt inside a chastity belt, or else simply a goddamn bloody cunt—fascinating but repulsive.

Anyway, emerge from it I did, don't ask me how. (Don't ask me anything. That way, you'll be able to let your imagination go. What more can I do for you? Look at my pretty face, look at my athlete's body; with pleasure you tell yourself you're smarter than me . . . and yet . . . those eyes . . . What if he's not as dumb as he makes out? No, that's not possible, look at me . . . That's it, get carried away, look for the secret!)

My first marriage didn't last long. "It's over, I can't take any more of your lies," she screamed, and would get so riled up her bones would protrude from her skin and her eyes would pop out.

However, she said this for a few years before she finally cleared out, taking our son with her.

What lies? What is it that they want? They're always digging for something. You can give them everything you've got—your balls, your money—it's never enough!

OK, OK, Babe taught me not to speak like that. It's my father talking. It's like I'm possessed by him. Every so often he gets inside me, takes over, speaks through my mouth, moves my arms like some ridiculous puppet. I have to exorcise myself to get rid of him, a job that gets harder and harder, more and more violent. And one I have to do more and more often.

I was single for quite a while after that. I got a job at the Road Forks Garage; that was enough to keep me happy. I was very wary of women at that time. This was when Internet porn was becoming available. For years I screwed around without laying a finger on any of them. No diseases, no hassle, all very refined. But all good things must come to an end, and finally I cracked. Babe wasn't the first person I'd contacted on the Web who wanted to meet up, but she's the first I actually agreed to get together with.

I'd never seen anything as gorgeous as her face. Same goes for her body. She wasn't a child-woman, she was a baby-woman. Her skin smelled like fresh bread; it was all soft with an odor that made your mouth water. I knew she hadn't been born just the day before, but she had that wide-eyed, innocent look, as if she was new to the world.

I adore women. I think they should fight for their rights—I'm right behind them on that. But the way these

14

modern women come on to guys, looking for a fuck . . . that makes me run the other way. If you're going to step into that trap, good luck to you!

Babe was different, totally different. We liked each other, and that was that. It's been ten years now. We got married the weekend after we first met. The boss let me borrow a white Cadillac that had just been checked in to the garage. I took her to Las Vegas, and we had one of the best Elvises for the cere-mony. A late-period Elvis—sideburns, swollen cheeks and a white outfit to match the Cadillac, the jacket with a big collar encrusted with diamonds.

His voice was a bit too loud, not as smooth than the original, but he had gusto; he sang "He touched me," which added something profound to the wedding—and gave me a massive hard-on. Every time our King sang and repeated, "Oh, he touched me," he seemed like he was a man with a sacred mission; it was as if Jesus, or Babe, was actually touch-ing him, and he was generously allowing us to share in his emotion. As he sang he leaned over toward Babe through the open window, then stood up and leaned over again, looking at the bride as if he were in a trance and about to achieve a state of ecstasy. Then the priest, a thin, businesslike broom of a man, had us make our vows. We slipped on our rings, then drove off.

A real nice wedding. I find that on a special occasion such as this, a drive-in provides both solemnity and sexiness. Every-one gets turned on in a nice car. You feel like you're alone in the world . . . Free . . . All-powerful . . . Isn't that right?

There were other cars waiting behind us, but ours was the classiest by far. We went to eat in a super Tex-Mex, then we spent our first night together at Caesars Palace in a luxury suite for the price of a motel room. It was an unforgettable night, as it should be . . . (Especially for Babe.) (Only joking.)

A man's lucky if he finds the woman of his life. I don't understand those people who get divorced at the drop of a hat. Babe and I, we've had our ups and downs. So what? I wasn't going to give her up for that. She's solid gold. We are of the same mind on just about everything.

Just about everything.

It's thanks to her I got back in touch with my son Tommy. She hasn't had a child herself, but that doesn't stop her loving other people's kids. We'll grow old together, my blonde lady and I.

At least, I thought we would. Before she discovered Carmen.

γ

Crouching down in the grass, her face straining toward the skylight, Babe doesn't know why that story about the hole in the ozone layer has suddenly come back to her. It's as if the sky has opened for her and she is hovering above the cellar like the eagle over the prairie, and what she can see is Bobby's Pistol, and his face filled with a wicked pleasure as he kneels on the hood over the girl's face pushing it down her throat, in and out, in and out.

A blonde goes into an optician's and says:
"I'd like some dark glasses."
"Are they for you?"
"No, they're for the sun."

Shirley Gordon's latest. Because she has hair like crows' feathers, she thinks it's OK to regale me with jokes about blondes. You can't choose your neighbors, and this one's a nightmare. Always spying on us and trying it on with Bobby. For years I've been wanting to slap her, insult her, dig my fingernails into her fat flesh, beat her stupid face to a pulp, scratch her eyes out, clean my toilet with her scalp, chop her into pieces with an axe.

Among other things.

Instead of this, I say really intelligent things to her, which makes her quiver with rage and run away like Lucifer from the Cross. For example:

"Do you know what the philosopher Pat Amodley said in his latest book, *The Cultivated and the Uncultivated*? 'Perversion or religion, voyeurism is a passion that can take on different values on the scale of good and evil, of the ugly and the beautiful, of the trivial and the spiritual. The voyeur is excluded from the spectacle by fascination, but is connected to its actors by identification. Secret looking can constitute an experience of trance. Of metamorphosis even. The staring eye, in its cruelty, chops up Time in transversal, transcendental slices. The edges of the body spread out, separate into gaps open to the air, through which the spirit exorcises itself, demonizes itself in the ecstasy of the fugue.' Not bad, eh? Do you know what the American Indians used to do? They shut themselves away in sweat lodges until they escaped from their own bodies and, in the form of an eagle or some other animal, explored another dimension of the world. What would you be, Shirley? A hog? A rat?"

To tell the truth, I didn't manage to say this at all, any more than I managed to knock her head off. But why is it that I feel obliged to listen to her, even sometimes smile at her?

It's weird. The girl Bobby is thrusting his Pistol into looks like me. The same face as me. Except she's dark, instead of blonde.

Apparently, our lot is built on top of a former Indian cemetery. Shirley told me, but Bobby doesn't believe it; he says if you think about it, the whole of America is built on an Indian cemetery. One time Shirley started making out that the dead were among us. She's nuts. A prick-tease. A clairvoyant who has to invent mysteries. If I hide myself it's to know the truth better.

I'd forgotten Bobby's Pistol was so big. How is she managing not to choke on it?

I, Babe, am in the shadows. Invisible. Warm, damp, dark. Like the night. And Bobby in the light. Exposed. I am spying, and my whole body is this gaze, in its electric, irradiating shell. Let the Lid of my Shell open, and it is I who illuminate the Spectacle.

"*W*hat are you doing, Bobby? What are you doing with your Pistol?"

"It's not a pistol, Babe. It's a dick. It's my dick, Babe."

*S*he used to be afraid at night. Of going outside. Of stepping on a toad. When it rains we are invaded by huge, black, slimy toads. They surround the house, silent and motionless, like traps, with their fat globular eyes and their repulsive bodies; they inhabit the damp nights, the invisible horror of defenseless nights. Who knows what might be going on when you can't see? What might you do without realizing it? What might happen to you? What might you tread on? Even in the best-kept gardens, the night is menacing.

Nevertheless, she did it. She launched herself into the blind world, she trampled the damp, secret, forbidden grass. The one known as Babe. Me. I am. I am the Night. The Night in me. Who sees my Night? Not even me. The Night sees me.

"Look, Babe, it's my dick. Look at it."

Babe, this so-called me who gets up in the morning, does all the things everyone does and then finds, by the time evening comes, that the days are too short.

Because even if she has been very active, even if she has worked, earned her hamburger by the sweat of her brow, *I* have done nothing, *I* have done nothing really Deep, really Personal, *I* have not exercised my Freedom, my Singularity, for there is never time for *I* in a regular day, even if she seems to be doing her own thing, Working Out, Seeing People, Thinking about her Career, her Health and Beauty, filling her void with the same things everyone uses to give themselves the feeling that they exist—which is nothing but packaged, sterilized shit that obliges her, Babe, to fatten up the pharmaceutical industry in order to lose the Bad Taste of her life.

Because she, a woman, never actually knows what being a woman means. Others seem to know quite well, especially men, who have very clear ideas about what they want you to be or don't want you to be: that girl Bobby is fucking and definitely not that girl. That girl and her opposite. Other women also seem to know this. You see women everywhere, on TV, in magazines, in ads; woman is represented in a very particular way, comes in clearly defined forms, has a very precise way of talking to men. Babe knows the user manual for this cumbersome body off by heart; like every little girl, she has always known it; yet it is as if she has to check the manual for the washing machine after every wash: you push the buttons, but when it breaks down you realize that you don't know what's behind them, you don't really know how the thing works, and you find yourself in a fine mess.

"My dick. What have you got to say about that, Babe? Do you see how much this girl likes it?"

A car passed slowly in front of the house and drove off down the deserted streets. It was a night in late April, already warm and humid. She had discussed it again yesterday with Bobby: wasn't the hole in the ozone layer turning all the seasons upside down? Nothing was in the right order now: the seasons were going mad and telescoping together as if they, too, were gripped by fear, the desire to turn over or have done with the good old days. Do you believe all that crap? Bobby had said. They had had a bit of a showdown over this, just for something to do. No, seriously, she was sure They were hiding lots of things. He didn't really give a damn, so long as it didn't stop him polishing his chrome and selling his cars.

Babe would have preferred to have an intelligent husband, but that's a rare commodity. And they can deceive you, as her first husband had done. Most of the time intelligent men are unfaithful, or worse, depressed. At least Bobby had remained the same cute, happy-go-lucky, uncomplicated boy she had fallen for all those years ago. Despite the strange look in his eyes.

"Do you want some, Babe? Do you want me to stick it in you?"

At first she had been a little afraid, like everyone is. That absent look in the eyes, as if he were looking at something inside himself, or far behind you, anything but the here and now. But that was nothing, nothing at all.

"Stop messing around. Just look at my dick."

"Your dick, yeah, I know. So what? Why's it better to say dick than Pistol?"

He was a fine boy, a real homebody, he wasn't interested in politics, he didn't go drinking in bars. He spent his free time doing odd jobs in the basement or smartening up his classic car. They ate dinner together in front of the TV, which was a stress-free way to pass the few hours before bedtime.

They would sometimes spend the evening in the little study next to the living room, watching DVDs or chatting on the Web—that passed the time even more quickly. So they never got bored and never took any risks: all Babe wanted was to hold on to her Bobby and her creature comforts, and he only exploited his pretty face and his strange green eyes to stay top dog on the Road Forks Garage sales force.

*C*rouching down in the grass, her face straining toward the skylight, Babe hovered over the cellar and looked at Bobby's Pistol. His face filled with a wicked pleasure as he knelt on the hood over the girl's face, pushing it down her throat, in and out, in and out. Stretched out on the pink Cadillac, her long black hair fanned across the windshield, her doe eyes fixed on the lightbulb above, her limbs spread wide, calves against the fenders, the girl suddenly looked toward the skylight. Babe withdrew behind the wall, her heart thumping.

Her body was churning with violent, contradictory sensations. The fear of having been discovered, sexual excitement, jealousy, shame, anger. She felt guilty and in danger. All these emotions formed a strange cocktail in the pit of her stomach, and it was ready to explode. She would kill if she could.

Bobby was wearing nothing but his socks, as usual. Babe was now hanging on to the bars of the grille with both hands. Too bad if the whore sees me. Let her say something, let it all come out into the open! All she knows how to do is lie back and let herself be screwed without moving a muscle, flattened against the hood of the car, her lips clamped round the Pistol like a vacuum cleaner nozzle. Under my own roof!

When he gets up, the girl lies there, spread flat, inert. Her mouth gapes open in a ridiculous fashion, as if it were still filled by some phantom dick. Only the restless dead become phantoms! She has the same face as Babe, more open. And a body . . . Long, slim legs, large, firm breasts, a bushy, plump pussy like an apricot. She doesn't move a whisker. A *corpse*. She looks completely stoned.

Bobby, the bastard, is bending over her. Delicately now, as if the whore were made of sugar, he slides a hand under her shoulders, another under her hips. He lifts her up, turns her over, lays her on her stomach. He parts her buttocks, pushes his nose in, takes it out, introduces a finger and . . . slowly starts to polish his Pistol. Not in any hurry, so calmly it becomes quite enervating. Finally he decides to lie on her, and pushes his Pistol all the way into her little hole.

Just like in the videos he used to bring home. At first, Babe liked them; you could even say they really turned her on. But she soon realized that it was always the same thing, and she would never see the thing that would really ignite her fantasy: two men fucking. All these films showed love scenes between women, but never between guys. The problem was she couldn't bring herself to *believe* in these women. With their honed bodies and silicone breasts, they looked like no woman she knew, not Shirley, not herself. In the end the only thing that excited her in these videos was seeing some guy in the corner of the screen jerking off while he waited his turn. It was the only bit that was believable, the only vaguely mysterious part of the whole thing. All the rest was just sinister, and Babe

started to resent it as if it were a personal attack on her integ\
rity and her beauty.

Allow her angelic face to be transformed into the muzzle of some dirty bitch? Never. Babe was born lovely and would stay that way. When she was quite young, she had decided to disguise her beauty under a veil of modesty. So that there could be no misunderstanding. And indeed, because of her physical appearance, people saw her as a paragon of virtue.

"*M*y dick, Babe. Don't turn your nose up. Admit you're mad about it."

*N*o, no, not at all. Neither she nor Bobby could have taken it upon themselves to tarnish the ideal image everyone had of her. In the end she became disgusted with sex, with all these lewd images that gave her such painful thoughts. These absurd situations and grotesque positions, the terrible dialogue, the guys with their bodies shaved, the women with their pussies shaved, the enormous dicks, the dilated orifices, the upright breasts, the stupid faces.

There was a time when I aspired to become a refined, sensitive, cultured woman. When I tried to understand art and literature. But I would have had to struggle against the whole world, and I didn't have the strength for that. There was a hint of shadow in my mind, a seed of renunciation, and I let it grow.

He's going at it like an animal, calling her names, grunting. She has never seen her Bobby like this; God, it's as if he's possessed by the forces of Evil. Babe is finding this painful, yet she also understands him: this slut's flesh is supple, voluptuous, available, completely subjugated; you could do anything you want with her . . . Could any man resist? Even a woman would want to . . .

And on the Cadillac, what's more! Bobby is crazy about his "queen of queens," as he calls it. When he first got it Babe would see him caress it like a woman—if anything, more lovingly. It used to belong to Elvis Presley. He had spent a fortune to acquire it. When he brought it home last month he was so overjoyed that, after spending a good hour in the garage fixing it up, he wanted to make love in the middle of the afternoon. But it so happened that Babe had an errand to run, and she let him down as gently as possible before getting out of there as quickly as she could.

Bobby's Pistol thrusts in and out between the girl's buttocks yes, yes, it's bigger than usual, he's even looking at it himself as if he is amazed by it, and at the same time his body is erect and tensing more and more, his whole body seems like a giant dick, stiff and a little twisted, it's as if gallons of blood have petrified in his veins, he looks like he is in pain, it's terrible, it's fascinating how he grimaces, more and more . . . He bobs his head, throws it back like a man crucified, closes his eyes, opens them again, my God he's going to bugger . . . His face contorts with pleasure, go on, go on, you bastard, you motherfucker, you'll pay for this, bastard, bastard . . .

*B*abe would rather she hadn't, but she couldn't restrain herself: her hands slid under her nightie, between her legs, where It was warm and moist. She came quickly, then came again when Bobby, with a quick step back, pulled out and shot his load, groaning, and with so much

26

vigor that the first spurt hit the pink bodywork which he had so assiduously polished.

She doesn't hesitate in the dark, it's as if she can see with her eyes shut. Her legs are trembling, drained of strength by the pleasure, but she is serene despite her urgency. Without a sound she closes the front door behind her and goes back upstairs. Finally her bedroom, welcoming as a womb. She slips between the sheets and pretends to be asleep as she hears Bobby's heavy footsteps approach.

δ

ello, I'm Bobby's mom. And this is Timmy. He's already been here for ages. It wasn't long before he came to join me. To be honest, aren't we better off here, in God's breast, than on the other side, namely the kingdom of Satan?

Oh, I don't resent Bobby for staying alive. He has always been weak, I guess he can't help it. All I'm saying is that if he were here with me now, like my darling Timmy, he wouldn't have this penchant for screwing with the pseudodead, with that foul creature. But you know, Bobby has always been a wrongdoer. A mother knows these things; I've known virtually since he was born. He was a nasty child, like his father.

Timmy, on the other hand, has always been an angel. A sweetie—quiet, obedient, innocence itself. And he adored me. These are things we can't control, and it didn't stop me loving them both equally, I won't let anyone say I was a bad mother.

But I swear that if I were in Babe's shoes, I'd take a large knife to his Carmen, without a by your leave. Lord, what have I done to deserve a pervert for a son? Bobby, my baby, stop this nonsense and come to Mom . . .

*M*om, please, can't you see I'm busy? I'm not a little boy anymore, you know. No, I'm not saying that to make you cry. But you shouldn't talk like that in front of people. I'm a man. A man has his needs, Mom. And Bobby's no faggot. It's like Elvis. Who would dare make out Elvis Presley is a faggot? Or even worse, that he's become a faggot now he's dead?

I think sometimes maybe he's behind all this. These apparitions of my mother (always at the wrong moment—but have you ever known a mother to appear at the right moment?). It could be that Elvis is prompting her: "Go ask your son to join us; I've got something I want to sing to him . . ."

I was young, and he was dead. I mean, he was supposed to be dead. I know, it's strange. I've often thought about it since, and I reckon in the end that the man I loved that day was maybe neither dead nor alive. I've kept this story to myself for more than twenty years. Who would I have talked to about it?

The reason I've kept quiet this long is not just that I'm afraid no one would believe me. Anyone who has had to make a difficult confession will know what I'm talking about. Elvis, I'm taking the plunge for you, you who were, and still are, great and free and generous, dead or alive.

It was the summer of 1978. To celebrate my seventeenth birthday, I had decided to go on the road, hitchhiking. It was the third day, I was on Route 40, just past Memphis. It was nearly nightfall, the road was more or less deserted, no one was stopping, no one seemed to notice me. The light was failing, it was as if it were taking me with it; I felt like I was disappearing. Maybe the people driving past thought they could see some kind of shadow, a faint silhouette, a ghostly shape by the side of the road . . . or maybe they saw nothing at all. If I had any substance at all now, it was so fleeting that no one cast a glance over to where I was standing.

I began to wonder if I'd be better off heading back into town, to find someplace to sleep. The few cars still on the road vanished into the red sunset. The huge sky was just an orgy of flames. Finally I decided to carry on walking straight ahead. That's when an enormous Cadillac loomed up behind me, drove past, then pulled over.

It had tinted windows, so you couldn't see anything or anyone inside. It was like a great pink hearse. It was magnificent, gleaming, caressed by the fingers of God, which filtered through the clouds in long, hot rays. I walked toward it. I wanted to touch its smooth, shiny, thoroughbred bodywork. But I just stood there staring at it stupidly, not daring to move.

The door opened, and I took a step back. I saw the dark shape of a man at the wheel and I got in. I recognized him straightaway.

THE KING! The previous August, along with everyone else, I had learned of his death. But once I got into the car and saw him, dressed in black leather from head to toe, tall and long and handsome, with his black hair and his chubby cheeks . . . The King, goddamn it, the King! I recognized him as surely as if he were my brother, or as if I had lived with him all my life. I recognized him immediately and I loved him more than ever.

"Where are you headed?" Elvis asked me.

"I don't know," I replied, feeling intimidated.

For what seemed like an age, neither of us spoke. The car ate up the road, which stretched ahead like an unrolled ribbon toward the last drop of sun on the horizon. I looked at Elvis now and again, and each time I was struck by his beauty. He was as slim and handsome as in his youth, even though when he had died he had looked bloated and gone to seed. Now, as he stared at the road ahead, I could see that he was older, that he really was forty-two. He had a serious look on his rosy-cheeked face, a determined, piercing, almost mean gaze that made him even better-looking. Everything he had been through in recent times—that physical deterioration from which he now seemed fully recovered, all his personal problems, the torment he had had to endure—no doubt the effort of coming through all that had etched this new expression on his face that I had never seen in any image of him.

I knew everything about him: his style of singing, his syncopated rhythms like nervous lovemaking, the glottal modulations of his voice that evoke the trance and languor of sexual pleasure, his swaying hips, the hypersensual way he moved his legs, his body, and also his mouth and his eyes . . . Like everyone, I knew subconsciously that Elvis was basically a sexual invitation—he came onstage to whisper to you, to beseech you, to scream at you: "Desire me!"—that Elvis so wanted to be desired that it made him the genius of rock and the masterful performer that he was, and that he had given to millions of people; he the artist, the sensitive, generous soul, had given everything, infinitely more than anyone could give him back, had given right up to the end, had given his life. That is what I suddenly realized, and he was still giving, since the mere fact that I was sitting here next to him filled me with such happiness that I ended up sleeping like a baby, my head in the crook of his arm.

It was his voice that woke me. It was now completely dark, and as he drove he was singing "Are You Lonesome To-night?" I lay against his chest, not moving, and at the same time listened to the pulse of blood in his body. Sung a cappella, the song was even more beautiful. I've always known that in his voice there was not only great charm, but also a fantastic joy to be alive, and also tears. The car tunneled noiselessly through the coal-black night, and nothing existed outside of his bare voice—nothing but our two bare souls within this enclosed space.

A while later, Elvis told me that I had caught his eye because I reminded him of Debra. He explained to me that Debra had been his first love, a little black girl with whom he had sung in gospel choirs. She was twelve and he was thirteen. He told her his dreams, and he thought he would go mad with grief the day she was killed.

I wondered how I, a white boy, could remind him of a little black girl . . . but I felt extremely flattered and touched that for him I represented some kind of reincarnation of his first love. "I love you as much as she did," I whispered. He stroked my hair with his hand, and softly began singing "Love Me Tender."

It all happened like it had at the start—in other words, better than in a dream, as it were the easiest, most natural thing in the world. My fingers found the belt and buttons of his pants and undid them. My face slid down his stomach, and while Elvis carried on driving and singing, I took his penis into my mouth.

His dick was heavy and soft and sweet as a baby's, as Elvis himself, and I could feel my own dick stiffen inside my pants, and I caressed Elvis's with all my soul, with both a vast maternal love and all the physical passion that little Debra had been unable to show him.

I was so extraordinarily happy that I doubted the angels in heaven could have felt anything so perfect. As the song ended I felt a gush of what tasted like concentrated, sugary cream spurting in my mouth. Almost immediately, I heard the King's resounding laughter, and once I'd swallowed I started laughing myself.

That was the first time, and the last. With Elvis, it just happened naturally, but I could never do it with another man, even if he had the same taste of concentrated, sugary cream. In any case, no one could sing "Love Me Tender" to me like he did, no one could reproduce the miracle . . .

Later, we passed through a town. Elvis pulled up in front of a Burger King and sent me to buy some hamburgers, some Pepsi and a milk shake for myself. We ate as we drove, laughing constantly at nothing at all. Now and then, Elvis would sing and I'd dance on my seat. Sometimes he spoke of his quest for God and I understood him.

As dawn broke, I asked Elvis to drop me off at the first bar we found open on the road. I knew I couldn't stay with him any longer. Hugging each other tight, *It's now or never, Kiss me, my darling,* we exchanged a long good-bye kiss.

At the counter, the truckers came and went, giving me curious looks, the waitress put a hot, steaming pot of coffee in front of me. I poured out cup after cup as the tears rolled down my cheeks. Again and again I could hear him singing: *"Shall I come back again?"*

ε

*A*t a quarter to seven in the morning, MTV kicked in. The TV, which had been watching them unseeing all night as they slept, standing in front of their bed like a watchtower, switched on automatically to the music channel. Until this moment the couple, normally dosed up on sleeping pills, would be burrowed into their pillows in a heavy sleep, a kind of black hole that sheltered them from the anguished chaos of life. Then the shrill voice of a female singer, the syncopated lowing of a rap artist or the obsessive beat of a drum machine would insinuate its way into their rusted minds like a trickle of icy water on the reddened, dusty tissue of their damaged brains. Every day and every night the corrosion advanced, unknown to them: it bothered them as little as a weathercock prevented from turning by rust worries whether the direction it's indicating is correct or incorrect.

Out of consideration for the patients who'd chosen this manner of coming back to life, the TV came on at a low volume. But as its mission at this time of day was to act as a wake-up, not as a lullaby, it was programmed to increase the volume steeply. It reached full blast within a few moments. Suddenly the noise was so deafening that it was impossible to stay asleep a second longer. Babe opened her startled eyes, grimaced and withdrew her head into her shoulders as if to protect herself from a bombardment. Leaping like Jackie Chan into a gang of mafiosi, Bobby dived for the remote (which was still within reach on the bedside table) and, without needing to look, hit the right button first time, the one that lowered the sound to a tolerable level.

Then suddenly they could relax, and they lay there hypnotized by the screen, watching unreal-looking girls, little whores jerking about in boots, hot pants and tiny tops clinging miraculously to their tits, leaving the rest of their chests, stomachs and thighs exposed to the awestruck gaze of the general populace. So sure of themselves, so arrogant that it was hard to imagine them having a love life or even a sex life. Dolls with sexy but untouchable bodies. In their numerous clips (the channel pumped out the same programs over and over), the girls were filmed between three walls of a corridor without doors, in a dizzying, claustrophobic trick of perspective.

Every day, Bobby and Babe lay watching this spectacle in a bewildered fashion for a few minutes, just long enough to wipe all traces of the night out of their heads and to remind themselves of what the day had in store. "Hey, Baby, hey, Baby, hey!" some blonde singer had been repeating endlessly over the last few days. Then they got up, hurrying without realizing it, as if trying to escape some undefined menace.

In fact this menace did have a physical form: Bobby's morning erection. That is why Babe, despite being particularly stupefied at this difficult moment of waking, got out of the conjugal bed first and left the room as quickly as she could, leaving her husband to deal with his daily encumbrance on his own. Once they got up, one after the other, they emptied their bladders, disinfected their mouths and made the appropriate gestures to show how pleased they were to see each other again. As they performed their morning routine, their joy and excitement reached its peak. The shower flowed vigorously, the TV blared out, the smells of lotion and scrambled eggs intermingled and wafted round the whole house. Happiness.

Together they slapped great shovelfuls of butter and jelly on their toast and drank bucketloads of translucent coffee. Life was full of good things.

Then she saw him to the door and remained on the step until he got into the Chrysler parked in front of their house.

He got into the driver's seat, started up the motor. They still seemed full of joy, as if the day were going to be a good one.

They exchanged looks: they found each other attractive, as well-preserved as peas in a can. Then a little wave, Babe and Bobby, Bobby and Babe,

"Bye-bye, honey!"

"Bye-bye, my bee!"

A tear sometimes appearing in the corner of the eye. Then the car slid off smoothly toward the corner of the alley.

At that moment she regretted not having made love to him the previous evening.

This daily separation was simultaneously a deliverance and a punishment.

And the weekends, when they were together, were at least as difficult to get through as the weekdays.

Babe would have loved to feel as one with her husband, but the fact is she only succeeded in feeling alone, even by his side.

*I*t's my fault. I've given up the pleasures of the flesh, I make no effort to add a little spice to our relationship. I'm cold, I don't know where to start, I've put my husband off performing his conjugal duty. Yet I used to like sex. I didn't need it as often as Bobby, but I did need it. Perhaps I should have taken a lover, to provide some stimulus. Or a mistress. With a woman, you know you're going to come. So they say. I've often thought about it. I've even almost done it. It was with a lesbian, she looked at me as if she were in love with me, it would have happened if I'd let it. But apart from that look she disgusted me. If she had touched me I would have screamed. I don't want a woman to touch me, and the thought of licking pussy makes me want to hurl. Oh God, you're getting old, Babe, you feel ugly, you're embarrassed by intimacy, you don't like yourself; in fact, you hate yourself. When you go to bed it's as if you consist of the single word "NO." Your only thought is to sink into sleep. Occasionally he takes you anyway. He doesn't abuse you, so you let him do it, you keep it as simple as possible, wham bam, for reasons of hygiene. First you pretend you can feel something, to get it over with more quickly. And by trying hard you actually manage to feel it, yes, only too late; thanks to your performance he thinks you've had your fill, but when it's really starting for you it's over for him. Anyway, you don't want to talk about it, you just want to be absorbed back into your black hole.

And so now, like in the mornings, he goes away, and you are truly on your own.

And you hate men.

They know nothing about anything.

*W*hen he came back to bed that night, Babe was rigid with anger. She wanted to roll over to the far side of the bed to avoid any chance of contact with this pig. But she didn't dare move. As usual, playing dead was the safest option.

After what she had seen, her body felt like it was chopped up into pieces. The slightest movement would scatter her all over the bed, small roundels of limb with the bone in the middle tumbling and rolling onto the floor, attempting to escape, and sowing doubt in Bobby's mind.

She was split between disgust and the desire to force him to have sex. That would be a good way to humiliate him, seeing as she knew he only had one round in his gun. But it had been too long since she had last woken up in a state of arousal and, in a lascivious state of half-sleep, grabbed hold of his Pistol like the mouthpiece of an oxygen mask. He would be certain to suspect something. And how could you predict what a criminal would do once he was unmasked?

Nevertheless, she really wanted to fuck. To feel his Pistol. She could picture that girl, that girl with Bobby . . . Shit! It had been good to watch that without being seen. Babe started to masturbate again, without worrying about waking Bobby with her movements. No more modesty, just the need. Once again she came with a violent jolt, like it hadn't happened since she was a teenager, when she had first discovered this miracle of her body.

Was Bobby still asleep, or was he just pretending? What if he had realized what was going on? Little by little the question wheedled its way into Babe's mind. She had never felt so terrorized, not since that day in her childhood, which she refused to think about. Terror was the worst feeling in the world. Babe started hatching plans to defend herself should Bobby try to stab her or strangle her.

She could already feel the push of his fingers on her throat, the thumbs digging into her neck . . . She could picture herself arching back under the pressure, her head thrown back . . . losing her mind as she lost the ability to breathe.

So she would have to be able to throw out an arm and find behind her bed some blunt object with which she could strike a blow on her assailant's skull . . . Or else, lift her leg to knee him in the balls . . . Unfortunately, far from reassuring her, these unlikely scenarios only exacerbated her fear. She felt giddy, faint, became crazy, then finally lost consciousness.

That's when the TV came on. Like every other morning, she and Bobby groaned and writhed in concert on their respective pillows. Then she regained consciousness totally as she always did—that is, exhausted, nauseous—but in spite of everything quite relieved to have crossed the vast ocean of the night in a single leap into the dark. She remembered nothing.

She performed the daily rituals in her usual mental haze. At this hour she was always on autopilot. It was only after Bobby had left—when, as she was about to leave in turn, she checked her appearance one last time in the hall mirror—that something happened. *I* told her that instead of going to work, she should go down to the garage.

ζ

*I*f I had taken pills like Babe, I wouldn't have been harassed at night by all these women. Ghosts, phantoms, madonnas and whores, holes, vaginas, asses, tits, mouths, strict ones, insatiable ones, an army of leeches clamped to my nether regions to make me shoot my load, from shame or sheer joy . . .

To me, the sea has always tasted of tears . . . When a girl wouldn't go to bed with me straightaway, I'd tell her about my mother's suicide, in a sober tone, and, with an unmistakable catch in the throat, I'd end on that phrase. It never failed. Women like nothing better than a bit of unhappiness. They'd throw themselves at me like animals do when they lick the salt off your fingers.

All sorts of people have found me attractive. But I am straight. Rock solid, 100 percent. Bobby's no faggot. The guys

I attract are after the same thing: a bit of muscle and a hint of unhappiness.

A secret and a weeping scar. If you have both, and you know how to use them, you can be whoever you want. It's not how you thought, Pa: your modern-day hero has a flaw. A large flaw, like women have between their legs, that's what you need these days to be successful.

But not as far as Bobby's concerned, no way. You don't have to be born into a people that has known suffering, you don't have to have been abandoned as a baby to bear the mark of unhappiness all your life. I'm not claiming anything like that, my ancestors were all white, well-off and educated, they weren't massacred, reviled, downtrodden, dominated, degraded, exploited, brutalized, oppressed by another class or an enemy nation. And I was brought up by loving parents, my mother didn't dump me in a trash can after I was born with the umbilical cord wrapped round my neck, I wasn't discovered crying in bed full of excrement after a beer can had been dropped on my head. These things happen and that's not what damns you. It's other people who condemn you. You should never reveal your weaknesses to others; they will use them to trap you.

No one gets a piece of Bobby. Bobby never complains. Bobby is strong. Bobby is solid, and his wife knows she can count on him, whatever happens. Bobby is a man. Bobby has a big dick and everything that goes with it; when he slides his hand inside his underpants to weigh it all up, he's got plenty to be pleased about.

That's why Bobby needs a woman on the side. A woman for sex. A man has his needs.

Bobby has his needs, big needs. And Carmen is his ideal woman. Always ready and willing to do anything. When I'm at the garage, I'm obsessed with her, I can picture everything I did last night, everything she took from me without flinching . . . And I get a massive hard-on and have to go to the bathroom and bring myself off, quickly, because I'm a conscientious employee and I don't like to waste the company's time.

Deep down, man is just a machine, with lungs, balls, a stomach that gets full and needs to be emptied, in a perpetual cycle . . . It's all mechanics . . . and every car has an exhaust pipe . . .

Ah, les femmes . . . ! Every man should have one, a woman who never says no. A good bitch you can keep locked away to satisfy your urges, who'll do anything and everything, who is always available and who is always satisfied . . .

But they never are. When my mother left us, my father thought she'd run off to be with her lover. Did she have one? A man on the side to attempt to achieve that impossible satisfaction? Whatever, it was the sea she went to, as if she wanted to go back to the continent of her ancestors, where they say women are so easy and light and happy . . .

The sea has the taste of her tears. Is Timmy bathing with her in that vast amniotic fluid? I cut the umbilical cord, I won't be joining them, I'm holding on to life. In any case my mother never really loved me. Her children were a burden to her, that's why she left, so there's no reason to follow her like that perpetual baby Timmy.

I can see her face, her large gray eyes; as she bends over me, I see how bright they become. Her whole girlish body sighed with pleasure when she opened her arms to draw me close to her, I was her favorite, there's no doubt about it, and Timmy would get jealous, would come join us to get his slice of the pie, and the three of us would hug with all our force, as if to weld ourselves together, and tears would roll down her cheeks, Mom, Mom, why are you crying, it's nothing, my dears, go play now, come on, leave me be, that's enough, let go of me, give me some peace, go to your rooms, go outside, I don't want to see you around, her voice became scary, we went before we got a slap, laughing, laughing our heads off, mocking her, the nasty mother.

For months, years, I tossed and turned in bed next to Babe, who slept like a baby seal clubbed to death on an ice floe, and whom I could probably have screwed without her realizing, if I'd had the heart to do it.

At first I waited stoically for it to go away, for the phantoms to let go of my balls so I could go to sleep. But that screwed me up, and then I had nocturnal emissions, so clearly the harpies returned to the attack when I was asleep, and when Babe saw the stain on the sheets the next morning she went pale, but didn't say a word. Awful.

In the end I resigned myself to solitary pleasures. Usually I got up and did it in the bathroom, a quick flick of the hand and it was over, but sometimes it wasn't enough and I had to start over again a quarter of an hour later.

I soon became addicted. I could even make it last without having to count to ten, using two hands like a geisha, bring myself to the brink of ejaculating, then hold back . . . In the end it was better than with Babe, and had the advantage that I didn't have to beg her to lend me her body for ten minutes, during which I'd have to try to satisfy madam without tiring her out—mission impossible . . .

I needed depressants rather than stimulants, but I couldn't prevent myself seeking out new ways to turn myself on. I was a total fucking obsessive. When I was single, I had the time to explore what was available on the Internet, on video, even on the phone. Enough to get off 24-7 for several lifetimes.

I started collecting videos around the time of my first marriage. I watched them at night, while my wife was asleep. But either she suspected something was up or she knew everything but didn't dare mention it (except to drop pointed, spiteful hints). In any case, she was mad all the time, and it made her look ugly. A clear case of a vicious circle if ever there was one. The madder she got, the more I jerked off.

So there we were, with a wall between us. Maybe I should have seen other women, but I was married, I had principles, still do. Unfortunately, she wasn't as honest as me, since in the end she asked for a divorce. *Ah, les femmes . . . !*

With Babe I decided to make do with my own imagination. No chance of her coming across that by accident. I had two or three scenarios I used—very simple but very effective. (What a great porn director I'd have been!) I picked one, visualized it while I pulled my choke, until the motor burst into life. One hell of a mechanic. Everything well-oiled, no breakdowns, no nasty surprises. Just had to think about it, and I came.

If only the female machine were so straightforward . . . I reckon with them the Great Mechanic wanted to do something fancy, something refined and sophisticated . . . As a result, not only are they complicated and high-maintenance but the system is constantly breaking down . . . And since they don't know one end of the machine from the other, they don't know how to fix it and get themselves going again. We guys have our little list of fantasies, sometimes just the one, and then just a quarter turn of the ignition is enough.

I know, they say that guys are having more and more problems with women. More and more of them can't get it up or have turned gay. But that's not a construction fault. We'd have no problem at all with women if only they were made like us . . . (I mean in the head. I'm not a faggot, you know what I mean?)

Easy to grasp, simple mechanism . . . That's the principle of man. Modern, quick, efficient, with the risk of breakdown reduced to a minimum. Then woman comes along, with her endless complications, and everything goes wrong.

One Saturday, Babe headed off to the mall, and I was doing odd jobs in the basement. By chance I came across an old supply of porn mags, which had been stashed away for years at the bottom of a box. Before I shoved them into a bag and took them down to the communal trash cans at the end of the alley, I reread them, carefully unsticking the pages. Spread-eagled pussies and erect cocks, faces of girls in ecstasy, positions, orgies, blow jobs, girl-on-girl action, penetration every which way, pools of sperm like condensed milk (or vice versa) . . .

Suck me, you slut . . . Fuck me in the ass, big boy . . . I know you like it . . . etc.

How does a boy stay pure when there's filth like this in the house? Shit! The world is filthy, man is filthy, there's no getting away from that. Only love can purify all this, but how do you satisfy your impure urges with the woman you love?

Sometimes a great sadness descends on me, more than a sadness, a misery as dense and solid as a stone, and to avoid being dragged into the abyss by the weight of this stone, all I can do is jerk myself off.

Satisfaction

Anyway, you only have to switch on the TV or open a magazine to come across images of sexy girls, with their up-standing breasts, their impudent thighs, their cheeky asses . . . Constant reminders of sex, everywhere you look . . . How can you think of anything else?

Delay the moment . . . That's what I did. Because I knew that one day my hand just wouldn't be enough.

η

Three short rings of the bell, then a breezy, high-pitched "Babe!"

Shirley Gordon. Babe sighed and went to open the door.

"Hi! Shirley!" she recited politely.

Her neighbor was trussed up in a pink lace robe. Where did she find stuff like that? Babe wondered. She hadn't had time to get dressed, yet she was already made up like a resprayed stolen car. She was clutching a yellow flyer in her chubby little hand.

"I got one for you! Must dash!" she prattled.

Babe grabbed the flyer. It was an appeal by the Church to the generosity of the faithful. In exchange, the ad promised, in large red letters, GOD WILL BE IN YOUR NEIGHBORHOOD.

"Hey, Babe!" Shirley shrieked ridiculously, spinning round in the sun, which threw a glittering halo around her.

49

Dazzled, Babe screwed up her eyes and stood still to show she was paying attention.

"Do you know what a blonde does when the baby's bathwater's too warm?"

Babe gave a wave of her hand, as if to chase away a fly, and turned on her heels. She hadn't managed to close the door behind her when the punch line came:

"She wears gloves!"

*T*he events of the previous night took some time to beat a path into her memory.

Enough time for me to reappropriate *I*.

I returns with my memory, then leaves me, I can't hold on to it, I'm too afraid.

Mom told me that the dead go to heaven, so I used to believe that Papa could see me when I was undressing or washing. Mom would come into the bathroom and turn on the light, and ask me in a suspicious tone: "What are you doing in the dark?" I didn't dare tell her it was because of Papa. I wouldn't have told her for anything. I sensed that would have made her really angry with me. She looked at my body, my breasts, my girlish belly. *I made you, so I'm allowed to look at you.* As if it all belonged to her. Disgusting! It made me want to be sick. To kill her.

But I couldn't say anything, show anything, think anything. Otherwise, it would be worse than death. A block of shame fell upon the room, the walls cracked under the strain, the house creaked and tottered, my body was full of cold coal, from my feet to my eyes, there was a taste of ash at the back of my throat, I had to empty myself out and burn it all in order to feel cleansed.

Satisfaction

* * *

There are lots of places in town where a woman can touch up her hair and makeup, straighten her skirt, check out her figure, the bags under her eyes—in short, the current status of her mobile femininity. The eyes of men and other women, shop windows, mirrors in bathrooms and changing rooms, rearview mirrors, compacts . . . All these are benevolent and hostile judges of this human being who is forever condemned to see herself as an image. God, protect her, her soul is troubled and her narcissism is contagious, as even men are catching it now! It is as if the whole world were a labyrinth of mirrors, designed to drive you crazy!

Oh, Babe had learned when she was a child not to admire herself. It was evil, it gave the wrong idea. Many of her friends strove without success to make themselves look like models in the fashion magazines. They simply ended up looking like whores. It was ridiculous.

That is not to say she neglected her appearance. She dyed her hair, because the blonde made her look softer. She wore silky clothes in pastel colors, tokens of her innocence. Although she liked her food, she watched her weight, because bulges were vulgar. She did check her reflection everywhere, but not to *look*. She merely *glanced,* and that was enough to ensure that her blouse was correctly buttoned up at the bottom and unbuttoned at the top, that her pants didn't make her behind look too big and that her long hair was all in place.

But today, when she glanced in the hall mirror, she was captured by the reflection. Her image looked at her from the mirror: Babe Smith, wife of Wesson. Her image stared at her with dark eyes, as if reproaching her for something.

Once again, her own image was looking at her . . .

But when had she experienced this before?

Something began to work its way into her mind, a nocturnal Thing; it was perceptible, close, she couldn't yet name it or recognize it, but like a mole it burrowed its way inside her brain. At that moment she felt a Disruption enter her life, the first effect of which was to make her drop her plan to go out, for no other reason than the sudden urge to go down to the cellar.

She phoned the university to tell them that she had a fever and was unable to come in. She had never missed a day's work, even when she was a waitress in a bar. The fear of negative judgment made her voice waver as she tried to justify her unwonted absence.

The frosty tone with which Kate, the secretary of the French and Italian Literature Department, replied clearly expressed disapproval, even bad temper. Babe stammered out a few more excuses and hung up. Then she stood there in the living room next to the sofa covered by a throw with a vaguely ethnic print, Native American no doubt, wondering what she would do if the telephone rang. But it didn't, and she finally relaxed. She turned to face the window, for she needed to allow some light inside her.

She wasn't really religious anymore, but in her childhood she went to church every Sunday like everyone else. White ankle socks, dark brown curls tied back, sermons, hymns, prayers. God saw everything and she always kept a watch on herself, for she knew that He only liked good girls, and how could you expect Papa and Mom to love you if He was not satisfied with you?

So she tried to douse the twinkle in her eye, to develop a look of disdain when the boys approached her, to not let her thoughts drift when she was made to say her prayers before going to bed . . . And she had retained this built-in apprehension of the Almighty who observes us, judges us and scares us with the promise of Hell.

And as she descended the stairs, Babe was filled with a new mystical feeling, as if her steps were being guided by God, as if God Himself resided in the basement of her house and was calling her down, into His Light that was like a Black Sun. God was no longer His Compassionate Cruelty but His Absolute Insensitivity, His Secular and Indifferent Revelation; God was there, and she went toward him with neither fear nor love, but with serenity and detachment, with a feeling of perfect Justification.

The events of the previous night came back to her, but with no negative feeling attached—quite the opposite. Bobby's actions in the cellar now appeared to her in their full magnificent, tragic dimension: Bobby got up at night to sodomize Death personified, Bobby did it to protect both of them, Babe and himself, he shot down Death with his Pistol, it was a splendid sacrifice and she knew, she knew it would change their Lives. Now she knew Why she had lived until now: for That which was about to happen, from this Present Moment that would never come to an end.

And she goes down to the cellar on a glittering Barge, against the flow of the Stream, except that the countercurrent carries her forward, and when she reaches the Falls, instead of going under, she will sail up to them to be Splashed in their white Showers.

θ

The natural hair gives her a wild look, more real than the shaved pussies of modern women. Just thinking about her lovely black bush makes me as hard as hell.

Women: I could have as many of them as I wanted, if I so desired. I'm not exactly lacking in opportunity at the Road Forks Garage. It's probably the thought of buying a car that turns them on. But maybe they're always like that, whatever they're buying. Even if they're not buying anything. Women today are uninhibited, even more than men. The mystery is: how come we don't all go out into the streets, to the malls, to the town squares, everywhere, to fuck one another, how come we're not indulging in a permanent mega-orgy?

People have probably never got off so much; they devour porn films, toys, all the women look like whores when they undress, they suck cocks as normally as they touch up their lipstick . . . But it's like we're dying to fuck even more. Sex, sex, sex. It drives us crazy.

Are there still people out there who think of things other than sex?

Women think about children, men too, we want children like children want toys, everyone wants children about the house, for the human warmth, because we're afraid of death, all that, but what about the children themselves? Do you know any adults who are at ease with their elders, their family? Listen to them talking about their parents and you'll see the look of terror in their eyes, every time their mother phones their faces contort with anguish as if they'd been trussed up and handed over to be tortured . . . It's hell for kids, home sweet home, it's another perversion, a sexual need . . . Promiscuity . . . I once saw a report on TV about rats. They swarm together one on top of the other until their tails knot together and they can't get out. They try to pull themselves apart, but there's this huge knot in the middle; they can't get free, so they die. Shit, I'd want to puke.

The Family. Frustration numero uno for adults, and a school of torture for kids, that's what I think.

If only I'd had different parents.

Babe and I would have liked to have children, like everyone else. But she had three miscarriages in ten years, so that's that. We got used to it.

I had everything I needed in my car, and I did no one any harm.

I love my wife, even though I don't have sex with her very often. I love my son, even though I don't see that much of him. I love my house, I love my car, I love my Elvis Presley records. One time Babe told me I needed to expand my horizons, but that's just storybook stuff, women's romantic fiction, they dream of adventure, but they wouldn't be able to tolerate it in reality, what they want is a guy like me, one who's always there, through thick and thin.

My workmate Dick will chase anything in a skirt. Women don't like his rat's face, won't touch him with a ten-foot pole. They come after me instead, especially older women, they are the horniest and the most frustrated. I have to give them enough hope that they carry on being my customers, or become customers in the first place. I butter them up, I look them in the eye when I talk to them, I watch them lose all their reserve, and when I sense that they're ready to get down and do it right there like a bitch in heat, I back off again, what a pro, it's like a slap around the kisser, they don't know which way to turn, then you act all cool for a while before you start playing them again, they love the torment, the whole movie thing, if you get them watering at the mouth, if you promise them something, even in front of their husbands, they can't resist, it's eating them up, they want to experience pleasure before they reach the stage when no one wants to screw them anymore, they panic, and when they're in this state they'll go with anyone who's even halfway attractive. Anyway, Ratface usually mops up half of them, since I'm happy just to sell them an automobile and then go and jerk off in the can once I've broken them down.

Ah! The sluts.

Oh, and what use is it anyway to let women get inside your head? It doesn't work, it never will. Deep down they don't like us. They'd like us if we were like women, simple as that. It's our dicks they're interested in, and they're not happy until they've chopped them off. The only way not to be consumed by it all is to be alone, as alone as possible. Parents, bosses, women, children, neighbors, politicians . . . money, work, TV, the law . . . Shit! They're all perched on our backs, eating us alive.

Only Carmen gives me everything without asking for anything in return. She's a good lay. And so nice with it. *Is your cock hard now?* she always seems to be asking me with her cute, pink mouth. She's so beautiful and I screw her when I like. When I like, however I like. I just have to open the case . . .

I had taken a day off work to welcome her. When I asked if we could go round the back of the house so we could go straight into the garage I had a weird feeling. I had to, because of the woman next door. But introducing her like that, from the back . . . It was as if I was sodomizing my house, my home sweet home. I pulled down the metal shutter, and I was locked in with her. I was already creaming my pants; she was ready to offer herself.

She was fantastic. She wore red lingerie. I could see her nipples and her pubic hair through the lace, which was as fine as a spider's web. Her long black hair, her juicy lips, her large staring eyes. I started to stroke her. Her skin was soft and fresh, her flesh supple, firm and heavy.

I laid her on the hood of the Cadillac. My two treasures. I undid her bra, slipped her panties down her legs. I spread her thighs. Her pussy, her bushy snatch . . . I dropped my pants; they were so tight now they hurt. Shit, she was good!

We did it again, then I decided to tidy up the garage. I put Carmen away in her hidey-hole, which she found very amusing. She was too good, too easy. Even today, three weeks later, that's the best I've ever had. I sometimes tell myself that if Babe had never found out, I could have gone on having it as often as I liked to the end of my days, in peace.

I chopped up the box with an axe, put the bits of wood and polystyrene into a bag and took it down to the communal trash cans at the end of the street.

Before Babe came home I had enough time to have Carmen once again. I just have to slip my dick into one of her holes. Within seconds it's stiffened up nicely and she sucks away like a vacuum cleaner. To be totally honest, none of the women I've fucked before can compare with her. Once you've tasted Carmen, believe me, the others seem much less tempting . . .

1

I talk in her. *I* talk into her ear, set off the words inside her, senseless, sensible, secret phrases. Words like bricks, sentences like walls, to stop the Wolf getting into the house.

(As a child she watched the tape of Walt Disney's *Three Little Pigs,* in which the wolf was drawn like a caricatural Jew. Of course, she wasn't aware of that. So it didn't really matter. Surely then nothing really matters, since no one is aware of what images show.)

Everything in the cellar was in order. Not a spot on the Cadillac's pink paintwork. If the girl had left the house, dead or alive, Babe would have heard it. She had listened hard enough while she was waiting for Bobby and after he came back, so the sound of the door closing, however quietly, would not have escaped her ears. As for the metal shutter of the garage, it was so noisy she wouldn't even have considered it.

There was no other way out, and yet the girl wasn't here. Unless she had hidden herself somewhere in the house. Babe began to hope madly, with a knot in her stomach, as when you're expecting to meet someone with whom you're secretly in love.

*B*abe stretched out on the hood of the automobile, legs and arms open wide, her mouth forming a wide O. She stared up at the lightbulb then, once she was fully in the role, turned to look up at the skylight. As from the outside, it was clear the glass was dirty. Through it she could see the light green of the grass and the darker green of the bushes.

And the darker green of the bushes.

Dark, bushy, like that woman's pussy.

If she hadn't been so out of it, she would surely have seen me, thought Babe.

She rolled over onto her stomach, her arms and legs still spread wide. She raised herself, lowered her pants and her panties and tried to find the position again. But this time she was shackled round the ankles by her clothes and couldn't spread her legs properly. But she had to know what this girl had felt.

Babe took off her shoes, her socks, her pants and her panties. She lifted her blouse and looked at her dark triangle, shaved along the bikini line to avoid any gross display. She ran her fingers over her flattened hairs to restore their natural body. Her index finger brushed her clitoris, but she resisted the temptation. She didn't want to be deflected from her objective: to understand.

Babe examined the hood of the Cadillac again. The bodywork was smooth and shiny. She thought about the Pistol. Normally I think about Bobby, she said to herself. Now, all she could see was this packet of flesh that Bobby had between his legs; she saw it as if it were disconnected from Bobby, lying on top of the car like an enormous jewel in a shop window.

Yes, that was it, it was no longer a Pistol, it was a Jewel. A jewel that came to life on, in and around the orifices of the Other. A strange jewel, a wild, primitive animal that crawled toward anything warm and moist, toward the shadow, into holes, a beast that slid out of pants noiselessly, without haste, with one thing on its mind, with its musky odor, its searching head, its moist eye.

A real Thing, screaming its reality, while Bobby was nothing but a lie, a fabulation, a deceit. Bobby, with his fantasies that he mistook for reality, his inherited movie screen, Bobby who was always hiding things. Who was always hiding things from her, son of a bitch.

And this deceit, this lie was like a darkness inside her, it was a bringer of death, it made her into a block of death.

She undressed completely and once again pressed her stomach, her breasts and her right cheek against the bodywork. Her sex felt as heavy as an anvil on which a blacksmith was hammering out a large piece of red-hot steel.

Finally, she got up. Her clothes were in a heap on the floor. She didn't want to put them back on. After all, she was on her own. And if there was another woman in the house, she was hardly in a position to take offense . . .

She went back upstairs in her undressed state and started looking in all the rooms. It wasn't a big house, so it didn't take long. There appeared to be no one else around. Trailing about from room to room in the nude like that, even she seemed like a phantom. But then it was her body that took up all the space, and the house had no more substance than a house of cards, liable to topple over at any moment. Babe started to crave company.

*B*abe, the giant sleepwalker, her enormous body weighing on her belly, condensed into her sex . . . It was becoming difficult to walk. Invisible threads pulled her slowly, gently, firmly toward the French windows of the living room. Which opened onto the veranda and the street. Behind the curtains she was barely visible. But she only had to pull them back to reveal the spectacle of her nudity to anyone who happened to be passing by.

She moved close enough to be able to rub her pubis against the wood of the frame. Before opening the curtains, she had the idea of massaging her nipples to make them stand up, but she realized there was no need: they were already erect, like two hunting dogs straining at the leash. Boldly, she pressed them against the glass. Then she didn't move.

The street was deserted. Bobby and Babe had to dig deep to afford this house in a quiet residential neighborhood; but she didn't regret it for a moment.

A fat child wheezed past on a brand-new bike. Jimmy, the neighbors' son. She quickly hid herself behind the curtain. There was no need: the boy was cycling straight ahead, crouched over his handlebars, his fat cheeks flushed with the effort. He didn't bother to turn his head to the left or right, knowing very well that there was nothing to see in these dreary alleys. Last week Shirley Gordon had told Babe that the doctor had advised her to get Jimmy to cycle to school, to stop him getting any fatter. You'd do better not to stuff his face so much, Babe thought in disgust. That Shirley! Always spying on you from her window or her veranda, ready to pounce and force you into conversation with her! And her awful jokes! What a degenerate, idiotic woman! And she was always flirting with Bobby; obviously she hadn't looked in a mirror recently and seen herself as she really was: frightful. That dyed black hair, which only served to make her look older than she was! Her low-cut dresses revealing acres of flabby cleavage! Her cellulite-ridden ass! Her ridiculous makeup!

Babe was still picturing herself bludgeoning Shirley Gordon's ugly face to a pulp with her fists and knees and feet when she heard a car approach. She briskly pulled the curtains aside to reveal her naked body, aching now with a surfeit of desire and disillusion. It was unlikely that anyone inside the car would turn around, either, but she waited nonetheless.

The tips of her breasts rubbed against the glass, and this tiny sensation rippled through her chest in gathering waves, communicating directly with her crotch, where she became a white-hot ball of steel.

The automobile arrived and drove past. Slowly. Babe could clearly see a middle-aged couple in the front seats. An overweight man and woman whom she didn't know. They looked straight ahead implied, like Jimmy on his bike.

They didn't talk to each other, didn't move. Their Ford seemed more alive than them. They looked strapped in like statues that the vehicle was delivering somewhere. They drove out of Babe's sight without the slightest flicker of interest in the world around them showing on their fat faces.

This depressing vision at least had the merit of making things clear to Babe: the girl was definitely there, inside the house! Bobby had simply hidden her under the hood of the Cadillac! How had she not realized that earlier, when she saw that the car was locked? She couldn't lay her hands on Bobby's keys; they didn't seem to be hanging in the hallway with the others. He had probably taken them with him, but Babe started rooting through his things anyway.

She found nothing in their bedroom closet beneath any of the piles of socks, underwear, T-shirts and pullovers. Nothing in the pockets, inner or outer, of the trousers, shirts, jackets and coats that were hanging up. Nothing in the drawer of the bedside table, apart from an old pocket-size Bible, a pair of sunglasses and a packet of tissues.

Nothing in the drawers of the bureau, either, or anywhere else in the study, including among the CD-ROMs and the books with garish covers stacked on the shelves. Nor in the living room, among the records and cassettes, nor under the cushions on the sofa and armchairs.

And in the so-called guest room, where no guests ever slept, not even Tommy, Bobby's grown-up son, for whom it was principally earmarked? Nothing, nothing at all. While she was upstairs, Babe also checked out the bathroom. In vain.

Downstairs, only the kitchen remained. No trace of a key in any of the cupboards. Not even in the huge refrigerator, which Babe searched thoroughly, for once without feeling pangs of hunger.

She should have thought of the basement straightaway. She went downstairs. It would be three hours before she went back upstairs, without success. It was the middle of the afternoon; Bobby would be home soon. What would he think of the fact she hadn't been to work? She remembered his heavy footsteps on the stairs when he came back to their room the previous night. She had to get dressed at least, straight-away. His heavy footsteps . . . like those of an ogre in his giant boots . . .

*W*hen Bobby came home, two and a half hours later, he found Babe and Carmen lying to-gether on the floor of the basement, wrapped in the ethnic throw that usually covered the sofa in the living room. Babe woke up, saw Bobby's petrified look and smiled at him. She was naked, like Carmen, whom she held wrapped in her arms and to whom she started whispering sweet nothings while she looked at her husband, her eyes glittering.

The trunk of the Cadillac was open. And Bobby had thought that his rubber boots were such a good hiding place for his keys.

K

The day that Bobby Wesson found his wife Babe and his mistress Carmen lying together wrapped in a rug on the floor of the garage, the rain had finally come to end, having fallen for a month nonstop, filling the TV screens with torrents of images of rivers in spate, flooded landscapes, people made homeless, so much so that on this first day of spring sunshine a new worry took root in the minds of the public, as they wondered what the papers would find to replace this daily manna of sensation in order to banish their Boredom, public enemy number one of the modern world.

So it had been a fine day. Bobby had closed the sale of an old Plymouth, a deal that had triggered contradictory emotions: on the one hand, he had felt like he was losing his mother all over again, but at the same time he had had the satisfaction of earning sufficient commission to pay off his two latest playthings, the Cadillac and Carmen, which permitted him to realize his wildest dreams every night.

The Road Forks Garage sold only secondhand cars, among which were a few antique enough to be considered collector's items and hence worth a whole lot more than the others. Joey, his boss, took care of the buying. He dealt with private individuals who wanted to get rid of their vehicles, and managed to snap them up for next to nothing by convincing them that they were nothing but old death traps, barely roadworthy. He then sold them at a nice profit, once Dick had checked them over.

Bobby himself was a skilled mechanic, and he didn't mind lending a hand between customers, giving advice or helping Dick. You might say Joey was an expert at exploiting everyone's potential to the utmost. "Getting results" was what he called it.

Bobby had found a sort of inner peace in his work. He liked to mess around with motors every now and then, and especially liked polishing bodywork and chrome to bring them back to their shining best after years of neglect. And on weekends he could devote himself to his passion: getting under his car, making it spit out its secrets, handling its oil-filled parts with the requisite skill and knowledge, starting up the motor, listening to it purr, the *fiat lux* of polishing, all those little acts through which he got to be on intimate terms with his beloved object and which brought him an idyllic erotic pleasure.

It was essentially an exercise of desire. During the week he practiced it in another form: dealing with his customers, which was a culmination and an excitation of this eroticism, as he had to employ his powers of seduction and sell himself as well as the car.

And once the sale was concluded, he experienced a strong twofold feeling of satisfaction and dissatisfaction, like that of a whore after servicing a client, a sense of both relief and frustration, which to alleviate he took a short time-out in the bathroom, where, to both celebrate and cap the deal, he unbuttoned his well-pressed pants and settled his nerves with a good ejaculation.

So that evening, when he returned home from work, Bobby had every reason to feel cool. He had earned good money, he had come and now here he was returning home to his smart house, fringed in gold by the rays of the setting sun, where his sweet wife and, hidden in the cellar, his hot mistress awaited him. He parked his Chrysler behind Babe's Ford, and as he closed its door he felt the first stirrings of an erection.

Tonight I'm going to take Babe out to dinner at the Kentucky Fried Chicken in the mall, he decided. Then we'll watch some TV in bed, and if we make love I'll give Carmen a miss for tonight.

Or maybe I'll have both of them, he reconsidered, feeling his crotch, where his sex was twitching at the thought of Carmen. One after the other.

After we've been out, she'll be in a good mood, he reckoned, as he looked through the living room window, somewhat disappointed not to see Babe's face there. (Usually, on hearing his car, she'd open the curtain to watch him arrive, then would go open the front door.)

"Hi, Bobby!" came the piercing, nasal voice of Shirley.

Bobby turned his head toward the house next door, smiled and replied, "Hi, Shirley!" She was standing at the edge of the veranda, looking unsteady on mules studded with multicolored rhinestones, which seemed to be flashing frantic signals

71

in every direction, as if she had the notion that her body was in danger and had to have these warning lights blinking away at the base of her being. Shirley hugged and fondled the wooden post in a lewd manner. Like some monstrous larva, she was squeezed into a leopardskin-print cotton T-shirt and shorts combo, her flesh spilling out on all sides, her helmet of black shoulder-length hair piled up around her porcine face.

Brunettes are better, Bobby said to himself, thinking of Carmen, as he continued on up to the house. Old Stan's lucky to have Shirley. But it doesn't look like he's enough for her.

He pictured Shirley naked, in obscene poses. He was sure she wore real stockings, with a garter belt. Bobby had an eye for that sort of thing. He could recognize them from the small wrinkles they made round the ankles, which you never got with tights, or even self-supporting stockings. And she probably wore rather enticing panties on that fat ass of hers . . . or no panties at all . . .

OK, she was a fat old cow, but Bobby wouldn't have said no if she hadn't been his neighbor. With her it wouldn't even have felt like he was cheating on Babe. She wasn't so much a woman as a thing, a concept, fundamentally no more than a hole buried in a mass of blubbery flesh. Besides, with the life she led, she was more or less a vegetable.

He wondered whether any other of the guys in the neighborhood screwed her. Whether she really stayed shut up in the house all day waiting for her son and her husband to come home. She probably spent hours slumped on the sofa devouring trashy daytime TV or watching porn videos and shoving things in all her mouths.

After we've been out, Babe won't be able to say no, Bobby fancied, one thought leading to the other. He felt very much in love with his wife—a fit of sentimentality in equal measure to the resolve he had shown in resisting the temptations of Shirley once again. I'll need to have a hard-on when I'm getting undressed. If I come to bed with a bulge in my shorts, she'll get the message. It might even put her in the mood. Tonight, my Babe, we go the whole nine yards!

God, life was good. The grass was growing, the trees were in blossom, flowers were popping out all over, the air smelled good, the whole of nature smelled of sex, of a woman open wide, hot, glistening, and tomorrow, Saturday, he'd have a quiet day at home, mowing the lawn.

λ

*B*abe planted her lips on those of Carmen. Bobby saw Babe's tongue enter Carmen's open mouth. Babe let out a rapacious moan, a sound Bobby had never heard come from a human mouth before. His wife kissed Carmen more languorously than she had ever kissed him. With her eyes closed, she ran her tongue over Carmen's lips and emitted strange groans, and then, holding Carmen's head in both hands, began to devour her with her hungry mouth, at the same time bucking her hips lasciviously beneath the throw.

At first he had wanted to run away, like a miscreant caught red-handed, but the extraordinary, perverse reality of what was taking place before him kept him rooted to the spot. Consequences and the future ceased to exist; there was no more decorum or embarrassment. Only the present moment counted, stretched taut between two galaxies. A precious, unsustainable moment, commensurate with that phantom body of the inadmissible now suddenly extracted from the secret in which it had been hidden, in pleasure and shame and the forbidden.

Bobby approached the couple; rolled up in the ethnic-print rug, they looked like a two-headed totem pole. He delicately lifted the edges of the covering masking the two bodies. Babe and Carmen were naked, their legs entwined, pubis to pubis, breasts to breasts.

"Are you going to leave us here?" said Babe in a tiny, imploring voice. "Here, feel! Our friend is cold. We should put her in our bed."

"Her name is Doll," said Bobby. "Carmen Doll. I'm pleased you like her."

He undid the knot of his turquoise tie. His head slumped and he buried his face in his hands and started to cry.

Tears . . . Tears ran down Bobby's cheeks . . . How beautiful! Babe wanted to lick them, then hurt him to make him cry some more, and then make him come . . . It was the first time she had felt this . . . This desire to give both pain and pleasure at once, which spread like a thick, delicious poison into her limbs . . .

Until then, her husband's pleasure had seemed like a strange, mechanical, vaguely disgusting phenomenon, bearing no relation to her or her feelings. But these tears, which oozed from the depths of an ancient wound, cleansing it and sealing it, these tears, she didn't know how, were of the same substance as his sperm, she had to make them flow, the sperm and the tears, that was the apogee of her female pleasure, that was the base of his male weakness, in this spurting, flowing abandon, therein lay her omnipotence, therein lay his surrender, and that's how she wanted it, how they wanted it, Carmen and she, in their perdition . . .

* * *

*I*t took some time, and a lot of effort, to carry Carmen from the cellar to the top floor. Babe held her round her ankles, Bobby walked up the stairs backward, his arms under those of the sleeping beauty, his hands under her bosom. The inertia and fragility of her body made it feel very heavy. They were concerned that the slightest wound might open up, run across her skin, split it wide open in an instant—then Carmen would disintegrate like Poe's House of Usher.

Bobby and Babe took great care not to bump her against the edge of the steps. Babe, positioned between Carmen's legs, looked like she was pushing a wheelbarrow, and Bobby, walking with slow, measured steps, encumbered by the mass hanging in front of him, with his tired, serious features, his hands crossed and bearing the weight of heavy breasts, looked like a pregnant woman.

When they reached the ground floor they agreed to take a rest, and laid the young woman carefully on the floor. During this pause, neither of them took their eyes off her. It was a way of closing them, of not having to look at each other or inside themselves.

*C*armen sat enthroned in the middle of their bed, naked, resting comfortably against the pink pillows. Kneeling down beside her, Babe and Bobby dusted her body lovingly with powder puffs. Carmen smiled, her lips parted. Babe had tied Carmen's hair, and the ends of her dark plaits dangled over the tips of her breasts. She looked like a little girl or a squaw.

Babe had slipped on a plum-colored robe. Bobby had taken off the jacket of his navy-blue suit. In spite of the anti-perspirant he applied to his armpits every morning, there were large sweat rings under the arms of his sky-blue shirt.

"I'll take care of her," said Babe. "Go have a shower, would you, dear?"

Meant to last for forty-eight hours, according to the ad, which shows an action hero bounding around a smelting plant full of blazing furnaces, only to emerge as fresh as mentholated chewing gum to embrace some cute chick whose nostrils flare lovingly right next to his sudiferous glands . . .

Bobby watched Babe, completely absorbed by Carmen—Carmen, entirely free of bodily odors. He felt a sort of dizziness, like at night when you dream you are suddenly falling into a bottomless pit, and the sensation of falling wakes you up. Babe was fondling his mistress with a tenderness he hadn't seen before, powdering her in all her folds, as if she were a baby.

Bobby left the room without a word. His wife scarcely seemed to notice. He raised the seat, opened his fly and pissed. The sound burbled through the house like the noise of a waterfall.

When he walked back past the bedroom door he saw that Babe had closed it. He hesitated for a moment, then decided to open it, in a casual manner, as if he'd forgotten to take a change of underwear. Silently he took a step back to make his entrance look more natural, walked straight to the door and pushed on the knob.

Babe had locked it.

"Babe, darling, could you open the door? I need some fresh socks."

"Oh, later, if you wouldn't mind . . . We're having a little rest . . ."

Her voice sounded so strange Bobby almost believed it was Carmen who had responded.

"Everything OK, Babe?"

"Yes, yes. Leave us alone, please. Just give us five minutes . . ."

Bobby went into the bathroom, threw his dirty under-wear forcefully into the plastic laundry basket and dropped his pants on the floor, rather than folding them neatly over the back of the chair, as he usually did. Then he closed the shower door behind him.

If anyone had been there in that bathroom just then, they would have witnessed, through the steam and the frosted glass of the shower door, Bobby Wesson spending a no doubt inor-dinate amount of time washing, rinsing and rewashing him-self, despite the hole in the ozone layer and all the ecological problems caused by overconsumption of water, especially hot water . . . But Bobby wanted to cleanse himself to the bone, more than that, completely scour his brain . . . and—why not?—wipe it clean of the memory.

μ

One ... Two ... Three ... Four ... Five ... Six ... Seven ... Eight ... Each wave was powerful, deep ... slow ... Each time, Babe felt the flesh of her vagina grip tight like a vise around her two fingers, and as she bucked like a prisoner in the electric chair, she counted the peaks, amazed at her performance, she who had never experienced such climaxes, either alone or with another person.

On the other side of the wall the shower flowed, interminably, and this lulling sound was the best sound in the world. Oh God, Oh God, make it last forever, Babe thought in her confusion, drowning in her ecstasy, looking at the body of the naked woman next to her with a blissful smile.

Then the water stopped running, and Babe raised herself and bent over toward Carmen, whispered some words in her ear while stroking her forehead and her hair, planted a kiss on her lips and headed to the closet.

"God has sent her to us," she said when Bobby appeared in the doorway, wrapped in his white flannel robe.

The night was dark, full of suspended waters and subterranean veins. Lying on her side in the fetal position, sucking her thumb, her hair untied, Carmen was sleeping. So Babe had placed her in the center of the bed, having dressed her in a white nightshirt with long Liberty sleeves. Her right arm, lying on top of the comforter, looked so charming as it formed an acute angle between her shoulder and her mouth, in which her digit was planted.

"It's *you* that God sent me," replied Bobby.

"No, no. What I'm trying to say is that God sent her to *us*. Do you know what I mean?"

"I know that I love you and I want you . . ."

Babe saw him come toward her, his erect penis (cut like that of every good American) about to poke its head through the gap in his robe.

"Wait," she said, evasively. "Let her rest for a while. Poor dear! Look at her sleeping there! I'm hungry. Do you want something?" she added when she was no more than one step away from the stairs.

"That's fine. I don't want to cook either," said Bobby, after they had made their ritual sacrifice to their health by taking their garlic capsules. "Would you like some jelly on your peanut butter?"

Babe looked pensively at her large slice of bread, as if picturing the scene in advance, then exclaimed:

"Bobby! What a good idea! I'd never have thought of that."

"We could add some raisins . . ."

"Oh yes! And some chocolate!" she salivated, feverishly pushing back her chair to go raid the refrigerator and the cupboards.

"Are you serious?" Bobby asked worriedly when he saw her return with her arms full of various dangerous cocktails of carbohydrates and saturated fats. "I was only joking, you know . . . We saw it the other day on *Columbo,* do you remember? Jelly on top of peanut butter . . . Maybe you were already asleep."

"Whatever, my sweet, I like it."

With a beaming smile, her eyes wide with excitement, she placed thick squares of chocolate on the layer of raisins crammed on top of the blueberry jelly spread on the coating of peanut butter which she had smeared on her slab of bread, itself endowed with fats and preservatives, white, soft and square like a fat compress.

"What I mean is . . . are you going to eat that?"

"Hmmm . . . ," she mumbled inarticulately, her mouth full on the inside and smeared with food on the outside.

"Not worried about your figure, then? Glad to hear it!" said Bobby, apparently thinking the exact opposite.

"You've always fantasized about big women, haven't you? Shirley, for example." (As she spoke, she spat multicolored gobbets of saliva from her mouth.) "And anyway, you don't need two thin women in the house . . . pass me another beer, please . . ."

"Which Shirley?" he said quietly, as if to himself.

He moved his hand under the table, rested it on his wife's thigh, slid it up the inside . . .

Her fingers covered in chocolate, Babe continued to battle with her monster sandwich, as responsive to his touch as if she

83

had been amputated below the waist. Bobby's hand continued on its way. Her thighs were already open—since she had started eating, she had adopted a totally slovenly posture: her shoulders hunched, her face and hands all sticky, her plum-colored robe increasingly stained and flapping open in shameless fashion to reveal her bare breasts.

"Aren't you hungry?" she finally muttered, as her husband's fingers began to ferret through virgin forest at the height of the rainy season.

And without interrupting her eating, she began to sigh— "Ah! Ah!"—breathlessly, her eyes turned up like those of a madwoman.

$\mathcal{W}$hen they returned to their room, with full stomachs, Bobby was shocked to discover Carmen in the middle of the bed, still lying in the same position—with her knees pulled up—but *on the other side of the mattress.* He turned toward Babe, who was standing in the doorway, gazing tenderly and admiringly at Carmen.

He looked at Carmen again. When they had left her, the comforter was pulled up over her. Now her nightdress was unbuttoned, revealing one of her breasts.

Babe hadn't moved from the kitchen. He didn't say anything. Probably he was just a little on edge, due to the fact that his overtures toward his wife had so far failed. He thought he had made her come with his fingers, but since she had continued eating without seeming to be aware of what he was doing, he was no longer sure of anything. And when he had tried to be a little bolder, she had undressed without compunction. Now he didn't know how he was supposed to behave.

V

The rain began to fall again. It'll never end, thought Babe. And this thought filled her with peace. The rain sputtered in the night that enveloped the house, and it was as if the whole of nature were lulling them, Babe and Bobby, as they lay against this personification of pleasure, this Carmen that God had placed in the center of their queen-size bed.

Babe had closed every gap in the room so tightly that the room was completely black, a solid block of shadows. They lay on their backs in silence, on either side of Carmen, frozen in some nameless expectation, their mouths open as if their very breathing frightened them. And like a butterfly emerging from its chrysalis, the phantom vessel of the bed slowly shed its skin and spread its wings with an imperceptible rustle, ready to leave the dark weightiness of its previous life to sail away in the blue sky with its flashing stars, to the other side of the world, the other side of the night and of the closed eyelids, into the eternal light of the inside, the light that the mirrors drink in as soon as one opens one's eyes.

The night itself acted as their eyelids, the black night and the rain, erasing the world with its incessant sound. And their dilated, staring pupils were now the all-pervading, fractal shadow in its entirety.

They lay there without moving for a long time, allowing the vessel to drift into a cathartic nonplace, allowing every atom of their organism to float in the magma, their bodies to unwind, spread out and dissolve into the general expansion of time and space. Then their beings, scattered to the four winds, began to reassemble, to concentrate and tighten in the remorseless stirrings of desire. And then, as if opening a door to flee a murderer, Babe made a move. Her hand slipped over between the comforter and Carmen's body in search of Bobby's Pistol.

It was still raining. The water from the previous rainfall had had no time to drain away before the rain had started again. Tomorrow, thousands of people would be splashing through water once more and the lawn in front of the house would be soaked.

Bobby felt Babe's fingers brush against his dick, probing it, before finally gripping it tightly as if she were hanging on to the rail of a bridge above a swollen river that was sweeping everything away, even threatening to submerge the bridge itself in its powerful, muddy current. Babe sighed. The Pistol stiffened in her hand.

If God had wanted to make things easier, He would definitely have made the Pistol detachable, so that you could just take it away with you and enjoy it at your leisure, like a snack. Instead, He had sadistically hung this tempting serpent between man's legs to force women to get on their knees and abase themselves before him.

If men had their penises in the middle of their faces—in place of their noses, for example—that would change everything. For a start, they would lie a lot less. And then they would have to prostrate themselves in order to screw women. Or allow women to sit on their faces. And if women also had their sex where their noses are? It would be hard for people to look at one another—you wouldn't be able to think of anything else! You would be able to watch yourself making love in close-up, with your sex organs right in front of your eyes . . . You could lick yourself at the same time: men could suck themselves off, and women could make themselves come by applying a good, chunky lipstick in an up-and-down direction . . .

"Hmm, hmm," groaned Bobby as Babe's hand moved up and down firmly, albeit dreamily, and then "Umph, umph" and the occasional "Ohh . . . !" Meanwhile, Babe said to herself: We ought to be able to move his penis around every now and then, stick it in the small of his back or in one of his hands, it would be less monotonous, more fun . . .

"Oooh . . . ," moaned Bobby in a more plaintive tone, his Pistol as big and hard as a cannon now. Babe's arm was beginning to hurt. She loosened her grip, and Bobby took advantage of this to turn over and clamber over Carmen toward his wife.

"No," she said. "Not me—her!"

It was still raining, and the rain whispered constantly: "Mingle together, my children, flow away, love . . . go on, my children, go on, I'll look after you . . ." Nothing else existed now but the rain, the night and the beached bodies, with a world to make afresh . . . The three bodies grappled together in the dark.

Babe raised Carmen's nightdress, opened her legs and slid Bobby's penis into her silky, elastic vagina. At the heart of the darkened room, with its supple, pulpy forms, her body was alive, passive, available, exciting. Babe had pulled her nightgown over her head, and, naked and pressed against his back with her pubis jammed like a sucker between his buttocks, she embraced Bobby tightly, pushing with each of his thrusts between Carmen's legs as if she were penetrating her herself.

"Take it gently, darling," she whispered. "Make it last . . . She adores that . . . Go on, push all the way in now . . . Oh, she likes that . . . You are so handsome, my darling . . . I like feeling you fuck her . . . I love that . . . I love you fucking this woman . . . My darling . . . If you knew what we got up to earlier, the two of us . . . I sat on her face . . . Is that a sin, Bobby?"

Bobby wondered whether he should reply, but as he wasn't too sure he could maintain his erection, he decided to concentrate on the task at hand.

"Is it a sin to do that on her face? The Good Lord has granted me pleasure, so it can't be bad, can it?"

If only he could have foreseen this situation that Carmen had gotten him into! My father was right, basically, thought Bobby. And as he felt himself starting to go limp, he closed his eyes and desperately tried to summon up some erotic scene, at the same time doubling the rhythm of his thrusts.

"I'll show you . . . ," said Babe, excited by his passion. "It's what I'm doing against you now . . . I'm rubbing my button . . . I'm rubbing it, it's so sensitive . . . ! She has awoken me . . .

the Good Lord has sent her to awaken me . . . It's as if I've been asleep for ages and forgotten all about it . . . It is so sensitive . . . I never knew . . . I never knew . . . It's good to remember . . . She's a woman, like me, do you understand?"

Just don't think it: *I'll never understand women* . . .

"She knows what's good for me . . . Women know . . . I also know what she needs . . . Her face, her mouth . . . I'd like to have it between my legs all the time . . . Have her do it to me all the time . . . Between women it's not a sin, is it? Even the Good Lord likes women doing it between themselves . . ."

The slut!

"Because that's what it's like in heaven . . . I came, I couldn't stop coming . . . How can you stop yourself when you know how good it is?"

The slut, the slut . . . !

"Oh, when I think about it, it makes me angry . . . You can't stop yourself, eh, Bobby? That's why you got Carmen . . . Now there are the three of us, I don't want it to stop ever, ever . . . Why does that make me angry? I'm angry, I want to come . . . Fuck her, real deep, avenge me . . . I want to make you come to your very roots . . . I don't know what's happening to me . . ."

Me neither . . .

"I'm a real bitch in heat . . . I love it when you fuck her . . . When you fuck with her . . . and I fuck you . . . Fuck her for me, Bobby . . . I'm fucking you . . . I'm fucking you . . ."

And as Bobby pumped away manfully, unquestioningly, Babe brought her mouth next to his ear and whispered, separating each word with the anguished precision of someone delivering her dying words:

"I'm going to tell you . . . the truth . . . I am a bitch. You are a dog. We are bitches. We want to fornicate. Uh! Uh!

Fornicate. I am also a dog. You're the dog, Bobby, and you're the bitch . . . Uh! Uh!"

Don't listen. You'll never come if you listen to this.

In the complete darkness the words had mass, they felt like objects hurtling into him, dark, heavy objects bombarding him through the thick curtain of rain. Under Babe's heavy blows he pressed even more against Carmen, whose breasts flattened softly under his sweating torso. He felt the sperm rising; he stopped still and held it back. As she ground against his ass, he heard Babe's deep breathing give way to high-pitched yelps. He surrendered all his remaining will and gave in to the pleasure as if in a dream, inside Carmen's soft, tight vagina.

ξ

Her left arm was as hard, heavy and cold as stone. It was the first thing she felt, even before she opened her eyes. She didn't move a muscle, for she knew the slightest movement would release her circulation and she would have that uncomfortable sensation of feeling the blood flowing back into her frozen veins.

Vegetating in her half-asleep state, she immersed herself completely in thinking about her numb arm, this arm that could just as easily belong to Carmen. Babe had Carmen's arm and Carmen had Babe's arm, a flesh-and-blood arm with which, now that Babe's whole body was paralyzed in a state of mineral well-being, Carmen had grabbed hold of Bobby's penis in order to fill her hand with his morning erection.

Babe also allowed her whole soul to immerse itself in Carmen's body, in order to receive her hard, satisfying soul in return. For their bodies were now two connected vessels, two dens where, like thieves, their souls could hole up and stash their booty.

Bobby heard the bell and immediately came up with a dream to keep reality at bay: he was waiting for a train, but instead of stopping in the station, the train hurtled through, its whistle blowing piercingly. He started to run, trying to leap onto it as it went past, even though he knew that this was not only pointless but extremely dangerous.

The bell rang again. Bobby raised himself on his elbow and then gave a start, surprised to find Carmen lying there next to him, naked. On the other side, Babe sat on the bed and began gently to stroke an arm, while looking at her husband with an almost frightening expression of depravity. He had never seen her like this; she was unrecognizable. It radiated from her face—it was like she was possessed.

"My God," he said, "that must be Tommy. It's midday already! I'm going!"

But scarcely had he uttered these words when Babe took hold of his penis and started to massage it languorously. Bobby was unable to recall the last time she had done this with such conviction, the last time they had spent the entire night completely naked, that they had slept so late on a Sunday morning. And yet it was as if it had been this way forever, as if his whole life had consisted of nothing else, as if the doorbell had rung only in a dreamworld, a distant world containing everything that was outside the house, outside his sex, things that had never really existed, except as distractions on the way to this moment of truth, this moment where there was nothing but sex, this moment stuffed full of sex, which was also an eternity, since night and day, past and future would be no more, there would be nothing but a present swollen with desires and replete with pleasures.

"I'll go," said Babe. "Be a good boy and take care of Carmen . . . She's hungry . . ."

As she kissed her on the lips, she opened Carmen's mouth in the shape of an O and drew her husband toward her. "She's hungry . . ." He entered with a single thrust, straightening his back with a groan of satisfaction. Babe got dressed, never taking her eyes off Carmen's distorted, ecstatic face.

*A*fter they had rung a second time, Tommy and his girlfriend Carroll sat down on the steps of the veranda and lit a cigarette. The wood was still damp, but the sky was now cloudless, and the sun beat down. A strong smell of vegetation and rain-soaked earth bloomed like a monstrous flower over the whole yard. Shirley Gordon appeared on her doorstep, her fat flesh barely covered by a saucy black see-through number.

"Hi, Tommy," she simpered. "Aren't your parents home?"

"They must be asleep. Their cars are there."

"Asleep—them? Don't you have a key?"

"I lost it."

"My dears, I can't let you sit out there, soaking your behinds . . . Come and have a coffee . . ."

"No thanks," Carroll cut in. "I'm sure they'll come."

And as she stood up to ring the bell again, the door opened to reveal Babe, who had thrown on her plum-colored robe, standing there smiling and disheveled.

Ever since he had left home two years ago, Tommy had been coming to lunch on Sundays, either on his own or with the current girlfriend. Usually Babe made Southern fried chicken or, if the weather was good, barbecued pork chops, and from nine o'clock in the morning would be cooking one of her famous desserts, one of the specialities of which she was immensely proud, such as banana cream pie or spiced chocolate zucchini cake—a cake she always made in two tins so that Tommy could take one home with him.

Today, however, there were no cooking smells in the house. Babe showed the two young people into the living room and went off to put the coffee on, excusing herself in an off-handed way that rather surprised them. Bobby still hadn't made an appearance. Babe turned on the TV and told them:

"Make yourself at home. I'll need five minutes to take a shower, then I'll be with you."

Bobby came downstairs a quarter of an hour later; his hair was wet and he was dressed in sandals, jeans and a white T-shirt. He in turn apologized halfheartedly and went off to pour himself a large cup of coffee. He had rings under his eyes but seemed more relaxed than ever. Tommy felt like a ten-year-old when he was with his father. Instinctively, he felt a bitter jealousy toward him. He'd been looking forward to introducing them to Carroll, who was cute enough to dazzle a blind man. But not only had he and Babe forgotten they were coming, but he barely gave her a second glance, as if he had better things to think about. Sometimes men pretended to ignore Carroll, but that was on purpose, to be contrary, a kind of power game. But Bobby quite simply seemed distracted. Not even indifferent. He was being as attentive as his current state allowed him—it was just that, clearly, he simply wasn't there.

Babe found the three of them at the kitchen table, nursing cups of coffee. Bobby poured her one, and she started looking round for something with which to rustle up a meal.

"I've got tomatoes," she said, with her head inside the refrigerator. "Apples. Ham. Sausages . . ."

"That'll be fine," said Bobby. "Bring the lot. I'm starving. How about you?"

She dumped the packets in a pile on the table and sat down. Feeling uncomfortable, Tommy got up, set out some plates, glasses and cutlery, got the fruit juice out and set about trying to fry some eggs.

Babe and Bobby wolfed down their food without speaking, still looking very pleased with themselves. Carroll picked at her food, with her chair some distance from the table, unsuccessfully trying to disguise her annoyance under an air of detachment.

"By the way," Tommy suddenly piped up, talking to his father, "do you know what your porn-star name is?"

"What are you talking about?"

Leaning over his plate, Bobby bit into a tomato, and the juice rolled down his chin.

"Nothing, really. I think Carroll and I had better be going."

"No, no, I want to know. My porn-star name?"

"Yes. What was your hamster's name, when you were small?"

"Mickey."

"And your mother?"

"Karen."

"Not her first name, her surname."

"Short."

"So there you are: Mickey Short. Your porn-star name. The name of your favorite pet plus your mother's maiden name."

Carroll turned away with her hand over mouth, trying not to laugh. But no one seemed to notice.

"His porn-star name?" Babe repeated.

"Yeah, the name he'd use if he was a porn star."

"Then mine would be Dolly Balto!" she cried triumphantly.

"So you had a favorite pet, then?" Bobby said, staring right into the back of her eyes, as if they were all alone in the room.

"When I was small. It was the neighbors' dog."

Her voice suddenly seemed to have gone husky. They were making love with their eyes; they stopped eating. Their good humor had given way to a sort of dull, almost palpable impatience. When Tommy and Carroll got up to go, they didn't try to make them stay, and could barely even summon a "Thanks for coming" or "Come again soon." As soon as Bobby and Babe had closed the door behind them, they went back up to their bedroom, ascending the stairs slowly, step-by-step, as if they were carrying a great weight.

O

i, Bobby! Nice day, ain't it?"

Shirley was leaning on the rail of her veranda, looking like an overweight, somewhat indecent widow in a flimsy black outfit which showed off large portions of her soft, white, doughy flesh.

Bobby hardly noticed her. As he scuttled up the garden path, she called out in a cross tone:

"Did you forget to get up this morning? I hope Babe isn't ill."

"No, no," he said without turning round.

He got into the Chrysler and drove off without a backward glance at the house.

After the overnight rain, everything glistened all through the morning like the flesh of private parts, still moist and throbbing from the inclement caress of invisible hands.

The greenery, the houses, the streets, everything that was alive and everything that wasn't breathed and shimmered slowly like an enormous organ savoring its rest after hours of unseen work, after an oozing, pumping flood of activity. And now more than ever one came to wonder what the function of this world-organ really was, what body it belonged to and why, in this morass of macrocosmic and microcosmic organisms all absorbed in their obscene doings, there should be these sentient, ignorant, tortured beings wandering round perpetually.

All this water and all this light made Shirley Gordon even more languid, lascivious and antsy than usual. She had no urge to move, she was a creature of apathy who enjoyed basking in the shade, but sometimes her appetites reached such a pitch that she felt like she could shift heaven and earth to satisfy them. So she spent much of the morning drifting between the living room and the damp veranda, unwashed and undressed, feeling moist and bludgeoned by her instincts, stupefied by this almost painful need, beyond all conscious thought, to expose her charms in poignant expectation of who knows what. Then she decided to walk across the soaking lawn to drop in on her neighbor.

Babe had decided to prolong her sick leave. It had been a long night and she felt tired. But more than that, she couldn't bring herself to leave Carmen. Tomorrow, she thought. "Tomorrow," she had told Bobby. But that was just a smoke screen, for nothing else mattered to her but this present feeling, this feeling of love that drove her toward this blind object called Carmen, which nestled in the pit of her stomach like a tiny but painful pin, just as she, Babe, took refuge, cruel and microscopic, in the body of the one she adored.

That Monday morning she and Bobby got up much later than usual. They had forgotten to program the TV; it was the phone ringing that woke them up. The answering machine had come on, but no one had left a message. No doubt it had been one of their employers.

Bobby had to skip breakfast, though before he left Babe insisted that he help her carry Carmen down to the ground floor. Barely had he gone out the door when the phone rang again. She didn't answer. This time there was a message. It was the college. As Kate was talking, Babe sat down next to Carmen on the couch in the living room and took her hand to initiate that transfusion of their spirits that allowed her to remain completely indifferent to the threats being leveled against Babe Wesson, the employee, a person who no longer existed in this house.

"A doll, a doll, my baby doll . . ."
The woman's voice was warm and soft. She was crouching down in front of a stroller at the end of the alley. Her face was hidden, but Babe could sense it anyway, split in two by a wide grin, the dark eyes shining bright. Babe was six years old and she had never seen anything like this on her mother's face, *"A doll, a doll, I'll buy you a doll,"* the woman sang, to the little girl in the stroller, the little girl who had outgrown her stroller, a retarded child, Babe learned much later, for now all she saw was the strange face, the elongated eyes, the round face and the gaping mouth. How tenderly the woman spoke to her! *"A doll, a doll, my baby doll."* It was like a flute, no one had ever talked to Babe like that, with such embracing love, the strange little girl was reaching out toward the woman, as if they were drinking from each other, feasting on each

other. Babe pressed herself back into the corner because she was ashamed, she didn't know why, she shouldn't have been there, her mother had told her not to go so far from the house on her own, there was no one in this alley except the young woman and the little girl, both of them in a sort of radiant halo, and Babe, whom they hadn't seen and who was now hiding in the shadows, in the corner, Babe the guilty one, Babe who knew, who understood at once, who knew the truth as if she were God Himself: the little girl was going to die—Babe had to make her die in order to live in her place and feel that joy that otherwise no one, no one would give her.

Babe wanted to go so that it wouldn't happen, but she couldn't. "*A doll, a doll,*" the young woman continued to sing, it was like a playground chant, "*A doll, a doll,*" if I move they'll see me, the alley was bathed in sunlight, it was warm, Babe's head was beginning to spin, that's probably why she thought what happened next was a dream, or a movie, two bad guys, one running after the other with a pistol in his hand, "*A gun, a gun,*" and when the first one reached the dead end of the alley, the other shot him, the woman watched the killing, then he shot her and the little girl, looked around and ran off. It all happened so quickly and Babe remained invisible, since it was as if she were watching TV, the people on the TV can't see you, and even if they could you and they wouldn't be able to touch, that's why Babe couldn't be killed, in the shadow of her corner . . .

But it had really happened, the little girl was dead, and the woman, before she could buy the doll as she had promised. All these years the doll had grown, grown in order to take revenge. My hour has come, my deep, dark, black hour. What have I done wrong? The doll doesn't love you, Babe. You've been waiting for her all these years, waiting in secret, and now that you are brave enough to love her, you have to admit that she doesn't love you.

Am I ill? Is it crazier to fall in love with a doll than with a human being? Does the doll love me less than some stranger I might fall in love with?

Will I go crazy? Am I already crazy? Have I always been crazy?

It's the fault, the fault gaping in my stomach, like an earthquake crack. Love takes me to the edge of the fault, I can feel it at my back, trying to push me, the bastard, it wants me to fall in. The nonlove of the creature with whom I have fallen madly in love, kidding myself that it loved me, that it was responding to me with secret signs. Poor sick child! That creature can't see you, that creature is not a real being, only its nonlove can see you, hypnotize you with its staring eyes. And you run toward the fault, your heart full of joy, full of the lie, you run toward the fault without seeing it, without seeing that you are about to fall into the precipice gaping at the center of yourself.

At the beginning of our marriage, I was so afraid. That I would be seized by madness. That it would get on top of me. Promise me you won't let them use electric shocks on me, I used to say all the time to Bobby. Later, the feeling went away. I buried it in some deep part of my mind. Bobby also has caverns inside his head. He puts flowers in his.

Now I am sad, sad. I have seen the abyss and I won't fall in. Not yet. But I feel sad, as if all my blood had suddenly turned gray.

* * *

*W*hen the answering machine clicked off, Babe got up, went to the kitchen and came back with a tray piled high with breakfast, which she placed on the living room table. She handed Carmen a cup of coffee and they both ate heartily—until, that is, the doorbell rang, and she heard the creepy voice of Shirley Gordon, insisting on being let in.

π

*B*abe! Babe! It's me, Shir-
ley!" (As if she weren't instantly recognizable.) "Can I come in?"

The doorbell rang again, accompanied this time by three
genteel knocks on the door. Shirley started bleating again in
her high-pitched voice:

"Yoo-hoo! Baaabe!"

Sitting upright on the couch with its ethnic throw, her
left hand resting on the arm, her right lying in her lap,
clutching a slice of toast, Carmen was visibly transfixed by the
commercials on the TV. Babe had dressed her in one of her
nightgowns, which showed off her curves.

They both sat still as long as they could, hoping that
Shirley would go away. And as Carmen watched the commercials, Babe watched Carmen, staring at her as lovers never dare
to stare, and thought she was more beautiful, perfect and

desirable than any other woman—even though she wasn't attracted to women.

"Baaabe! Are you unwell? Do you want me to call a doctor?"

God, thought Babe, she never gives up. She ran her hand through her unkempt hair and tied the belt of her robe (noticing that it was spattered with grease marks). At first she tried to talk to her through the door:

"I'm fine, Shirley. I've just got out of the tub, and . . . I've got a touch of flu . . . I don't feel myself . . ."

"What's that? I can't hear you . . . Won't you open the door?"

"I said, I don't feel myself," Babe shouted.

"You're going to kill yourself? Sweet Jesus! Don't do it! I'll call the police!"

"No, don't . . ."

"Stay calm. I'll take care of everything . . ."

"Shirley, it's OK." Babe sighed as she undid the lock and stood behind the open door, blocking the entrance.

"Sweet Jesus, you gave me a fright . . . You're sure everything's OK?"

"I'm sure."

"Really? If there's anything you want to talk about, Babe . . ."

"No. No, no . . ."

"All I'm saying is, you can talk to me . . . We're neighbors, we help each other out, isn't that right?"

"Listen, it's just a touch of flu."

"'A touch of flu'? Is that why you were shut indoors the whole of Saturday?"

104

"Right now Bobby and I are pretty tired . . . We shouldn't have said yes to working Saturdays, even as a one-shot deal . . ."

"Yeah, yeah . . . We all say that, but the money comes in handy, doesn't it?" said Shirley, in her clucking voice. "And my poor husband with his two jobs . . . If you could see the state he's in sometimes . . . Can I come in for a couple of minutes?"

"Oh, er . . . well, the place is in a mess and I'm not dressed yet . . ."

"I could give you a hand."

"No, no thanks, Shirley . . . I think I'll go back to bed . . ."

"I just have a favor to ask you . . . Could you lend me your axe?"

"My axe?"

"Yes. I've got a job to do. You know how it is . . . A woman on her own at home . . ."

"For what sort of job? Chopping down trees?"

"Hee-hee, you're such a scream, honey. No, just a corpse to chop up."

"Well, the tools are in the garage. If you want to walk round the back, I'll hand it out to you."

Babe closed the door. Shirley came down from the veranda and, balancing on her heels, trotted round the house to the entrance to the garage. A moment later the metal shutter rose a few inches and Babe's hand slid the axe through the gap. Then the shutter slammed shut again.

"Don't be afraid, it's over . . . She's gone . . . ," Babe murmured as she ran her hands and lips over Carmen's face, neck, arms and chest.

"What do you think about that crazy woman, eh? She won't bother us again . . . How beautiful you are, my darling . . . *My doll, my baby doll* . . . Let me undress you . . . You are so beautiful . . . I'd love to have had a doll like you when I was small . . . You'll never leave me, will you? We're so good together, you and I . . ."

Carmen's skin was soft, so soft. There was no Evil in that body, lurking, ready to rise up and torment you even in the good times, no Evil would spread its canker into her limbs or her head, she was pure flesh made for pleasure, yes, pure, and in loving her you found yourself as if by a miracle, washed clean of all stain, for she accepted everything without complaint, like a Buddha or a garbage chute, Carmen, with her black hair and black pubes, her holes and her passivity, was simultaneously fire and ice, the Good Lord could not have made Himself flesh better than in this innocent and charitable body that asked for nothing more than to give relief to men and succor to women.

Babe took off her robe, placed her darling on the couch and began to kiss her passionately on the mouth, then over her whole body, purring like a kitten. She brought herself to a state of excitement, attempting to release the tension from her fight with Shirley. Finally, she got on top of the wanton body and lay there a long time, rubbing her pubis against that of Carmen. When she had finished, she started laughing feverishly.

"My darling, you're so good! I love you, I love you! Yes, yes, I know what you want . . . Don't you worry, Mama Babe will take care of everything . . . A lovely girl like you . . . Of course I'll bring you what you need . . . You stay there, trust me . . . I'll take care of everything . . . everything . . ."

And for the first time in her life, Babe left the house without having washed first. Her body smelled of love: no bad thing, she thought, considering what she had to do. She left Carmen lying on the couch, wrapped in the throw with the totemic pattern to keep her warm, and quickly slipped into her shortest, most tightly fitting dress, without putting on a bra and panties. Not bothering to wash her face or brush her teeth, she applied some showy makeup—blue eye shadow on her eyelids, large patches of pink blush on her cheeks, dark red, almost black lipstick enlarging the size of her mouth. Then she grabbed her handbag and decamped as if she had an urgent rendezvous.

ρ

*B*abe's breasts bounced free, and the spring breeze kissed her lightly on her neck, her arms, her bare legs and playfully wheedled its way up her dress, as she ran down the alley to her car before Shirley Gordon had the chance to come out and call to her.

She got into the car, breathed a sigh, then drove off. She had never done anything so exciting, audacious, subversive. For once she was mistress of her own life; she felt as if she had entered another dimension. In a great surge of adrenaline she drove to the mall. She was nervous, elegant and sporty at the same time; she would never have thought herself capable of that. She thought about Bobby and his love of cars. Now she could see why. Once you got your hands on it, this vehicle so easily became an instrument of power and pleasure . . . ! Wedged into her seat, she felt alert and ready to eat the whole world!

At this time of day the mall was always crawling with people. Babe preferred the early morning, just after it opened, when she went for her weekly jog. There was hardly anyone about then, except for a few other joggers who did a circuit of all four floors as if chasing one another from one escalator to the next. They formed a sort of confraternity, felt they were kindred spirits—people-who-keep-themselves-in-shape, or people-who-push-beyond-their-limits. Running all the way round the mall in little groups was exactly the sort of thing that, in the modern world, gave human beings dignity and enriched their lives, something Babe understood, but which Bobby, trapped as he was in the material trivia of everyday life, pigheadedly dismissed out of hand.

Now, however, there was a crowd of people of all ages, pale in the neon lighting, packed into the take-outs, filling up the alleyways and sauntering from one store to another, killing time with the help of their credit cards. Babe went into Pearl's on level two, and started checking out the rack she normally never stopped at—the one with the slutty underwear.

"Mrs. Wesson! Hey, Mrs. Wesson!"

Babe turned around and saw Carroll leaning over the counter, in the middle of paying for a white cotton bra-and-panties set. She was smiling and yelling out with all the naïveté and cruelty of her twenty years.

"Oh, very nice!" Carrol said sarcastically, looking at the garter belt in mauve lace that Babe was holding in front of her chest as if to protect herself; the minuscule matching G-string with the tuft of red fur on the front looked like a little heart.

"And so sweet . . . ," she added. "Bye, Mrs. Wesson. I'll give your son your love!"

Babe went back to looking at some tight-fitting bodices, lowering her head to disguise the fact she was blushing to the roots of her hair.

It was time to get serious. If she wanted to get this done before Bobby got back, there wasn't a moment to lose. Carrying her Pearl's bag in her hand, she went up to level four and headed straight for the men's bathroom.

She'd had time to think about it in the shop: where could she find a man quickly? In the past, whenever she had gone out she had felt that there were dozens of men who would have liked to sleep with her, felt it could happen at any time if she even once dropped her protective mask of dignified reserve. But today was nothing like her fantasies. No one seemed to be thinking about sex. They didn't seem to be thinking about anything at all, they were like automata placed there by a stage designer. And it was as if Babe were an automaton herself, as if she were invisible as a person, as a body, as a look.

She had felt this ever since she had arrived at the underground parking lot. The cars were all in a line, with their eyes open, their eyes extinguished, and the people who got out, got in or sat inside looked dead or false, as false as that couple in the Ford the other morning, when Babe was standing naked in the window waiting for them to spot her. It was like a nightmare where she alone had survived in an annihilated world, but it was also a marvelous dream, for she no longer feared anything. She alone was alive, she and the cars, the nice cars. However, she had to find a man for Carmen.

She didn't dare enter. She stood at the entrance to the men's bathroom and waited. The first to come out was a young African-American in a cap, tall, handsome and as meaty as a steer. Babe felt herself melting like an ice cream in the sun. He must have an ENORMOUS one! Babe herself had never slept with a black man, but Carmen would love it!

But with only three strides of his long legs, the boy had already crossed to the other side of the floor. Babe hesitated before deciding not to follow him; she didn't know what she would have to have done to attract his attention.

She stepped back to allow a large guy in a cowboy hat and checked shirt to enter the bathroom. He stared at her with a cheesy grin.

"Are you waitin' for someone, li'l lady?" he asked in a falsetto voice.

Babe wanted to reply: "I'm waiting for my husband." But nothing came out of her mouth. She felt angry and rather grubby. What did he think she was doing? She walked away, her legs trembling.

Yes, I'm waiting for my husband, of course. He is taking a piss—can't you hear him? You see, my husband has the longest piss of any man I know. And when I say "long," I don't just mean long in length. He can certainly piss quite a distance—he could probably break records—but that's not all. My husband is a stayer. He can stand there relieving himself for minutes or even hours at a time. He's a genuine faucet, what am I saying, a watering can, no, what am I saying, a fireman's hose! Why else would I be hanging round the men's bathroom if I weresn't waiting for my husband? That is indeed, sir, the reason I am here, waiting patiently but eagerly, as befits the wife of such a man. But now you mention it, he has been in there a good five or ten minutes . . . I think I'll go and do some shopping, and I'll be back to wait for him after you are long gone . . .

112

I'll come back tomorrow, thought Babe. I'll know what I'm doing then. In any case, it's too late for today.

She drove home, then ran up to the front door to escape Shirley Gordon, who was already twitching her curtain to see what was going on. Exhausted, she flopped onto the couch, laid her head on Carmen's lap and, grabbing the remote, turned on the TV.

σ

A suite in a large hotel. On the walls, numerous glamour photographs of an actress in her forties, none other than . . . Shirley Gordon! Dressed in her flimsy, see-through black number.

Shirley checks herself nervously in the mirror: hair, makeup . . .

There is a knock at the door. She applies a last squirt of perfume.

SHIRLEY Enter.

Enter a man, about the same age as her, slim, charming, wearing jeans, hair tied back in a ponytail. They look at each other with great feeling.

He walks over to her and kisses her on the cheek.

SHIRLEY Thanks for coming . . .

PAUL I guess great actresses can do that—resurrect ghosts from the past just by picking up the phone.

Shirley goes over to a low table where there is an ice bucket with two bottles of champagne.

SHIRLEY   Your favorite champagne!

She pours out two glasses.

PAUL (*Raising his glass*)   Here's to you, Shirley!

SHIRLEY   No, here's to you, Paul. I want to drink to you, to your success.

PAUL   Well, I guess we don't need to wish *you* glory, Shirley. Unlike me . . .

SHIRLEY   Please . . .

PAUL   I've had no news from you for fifteen years other than what I read in the papers . . .

They sit on the couch.

PAUL   You said you wanted to talk. What's happened?

SHIRLEY (*Troubled*)   Nothing . . . It's just that . . . I do have something very important to tell you, but . . . it's difficult . . .

She pours herself another glass.

PAUL   We've all the time in the world . . .

SHIRLEY   You know, I never thought I'd find you again so easily. I'd have come to see you at your place—it would have been less impersonal than receiving you in this hotel— but I thought maybe you were married and . . .

PAUL   The hotel is fine . . . But how is it to be in New York? You must be missing the sun of L.A. . . .

SHIRLEY   Sometimes I dream of my simple little room on my parents' ranch . . . Oh, Paul, do you remember going horseback riding when we were children? And when we hid in the barn among the hay bales? . . . How warm it could be!

I don't think I've ever felt as warm as that, not even in a palace . . . But I guess you've made a new life for yourself . . .

PAUL In fifteen years I've made three new lives. You can see it hasn't been easy. But this is the real thing. I'm married, I have a wonderful baby, and Carroll and I plan to have at least two more . . .

Shirley gets up, turns her back to Paul and downs a glass of champagne in one gulp.

SHIRLEY (*After a pause*) Congratulations. It's funny—when we were together you were dead set against marriage . . .

PAUL Dead set against marriage? Not at all!

SHIRLEY What I mean is, since you didn't marry me I guess it was because you didn't love me enough.

PAUL Are you trying to hurt me? Are you trying to hurt us both?

SHIRLEY I'm trying to be honest, that's all. Now you have a little wife, a baby, a quiet life. You're happy. That's fine. All I'm saying is that you didn't do it with me. I guess I just wasn't ordinary enough for you.

PAUL I must be dreaming! You call me here after fifteen years just to throw a fit of jealousy, for this display of wounded pride! Not "ordinary enough" for me . . . Please, Shirley, come down off your cloud.

SHIRLEY I am no ordinary woman. You know that, and that's why you never married me.

PAUL Would you have married me if I'd asked you?

SHIRLEY You never asked me.

PAUL That's unfair. You know the answer would be no. You no more wanted to get married than I did. The truth is, we were young, we wanted to pursue our acting careers and we were ready to sacrifice everything for that. Including our love.

SHIRLEY   And that's exactly what we did.

PAUL   Whose fault is that?

SHIRLEY   You were the one who left.

PAUL   And why was that? Listen, it was painful enough at the time. There's no point in stirring it all up now . . .

SHIRLEY   You're right. We won't talk about it anymore. You couldn't stand the fact that I was becoming more successful than you. It's only human. Particularly for a man. Women are more modest, they know how to live in the shadow . . .

PAUL (*Laughing*)   Ha! You're incredible, do you know that? Here you are in New York promoting your latest movie, in which you have the star part . . . Your face is in every magazine, on every TV channel . . . You shut yourself away in your hotel suite and plaster the walls with photos of yourself . . . And you talk to me about women's modesty . . .

SHIRLEY   All I meant to say was . . . OK, let's not talk about it anymore. What's past is past, no point in going back. You've never understood me . . . I'm sorry. I didn't want it to be like this.

PAUL   The problem is, you see, you think you know everything. You talk to me about my "quiet little life." What do you know about it? Have you asked me once about my work since I got here? All you wanted to know was whether or not I'd found a new woman.

SHIRLEY   And you? Have you asked me once about my private life? Have you asked me if I'm happy?

Shirley pours out another drink and walks around the room, agitated. She seems a little drunk or at least overexcited.

She starts to cry.

Paul goes over and embraces her to try to console her.

He takes the glass from her hand, sets it down. Then he takes Shirley's face between his hands.

PAUL (*Tenderly*)   Baby *Shirley* shouldn't drink champagne . . . Because it comes out of her beautiful eyes in fountains . . .

He begins kissing her tears.

PAUL   . . . And I drink it from her cheeks.

Her eyes still full of tears, Shirley places her hand on the back of Paul's neck. They look at each other and exchange a long kiss, mouths wide-open.

SHIRLEY   Paul . . .

PAUL   Shirley . . .

SHIRLEY   Oh, Paul . . .

PAUL   Yes, Shirley?

SHIRLEY   I love you.

PAUL (*Softly*)   Don't say that.

SHIRLEY   Why not?

PAUL   Because it's not possible.

SHIRLEY (*Plaintively*)   But I love you . . . I've never stopped loving you all this time! That's why it's never worked with anyone else . . . (*In a despairing voice*)   I thought about you, Paul. I've thought about you all these years . . .

PAUL   Shirley, look at me. You can see I'm not the same person. Neither of us is the same person.

119

SHIRLEY   I'm not asking you to go back.

PAUL   What do you want, then? Why did you ask me to come?

SHIRLEY   I . . . I've got something to tell you. It's very important.

She takes the second bottle from the ice bucket, fills the two glasses and hands one to Paul.

PAUL   Do you really think that will make it any easier?

SHIRLEY   I know what you're saying. The star descends into drink and depression. Soon she'll be a bloated madwoman whom no one can stand. Men will avoid her, even her closest friends will start keeping their distance, and she'll sit there in her empty mansion with nothing but her regrets and her madness . . . Kind of clichéd, isn't it?

PAUL   Don't say such things. It won't be like that at all. You've gotten where you are today because you've always been strong, much stronger than me. I don't see why that should change.

SHIRLEY   Can't you see I'm not doing well? Can't you see I'm not doing well at all? I've had too much in my life. Too many affairs, too many men, too much success, too much money, too much travel. I've had enough of being a capricious little girl. I want to be a real woman.

PAUL   I understand. I once looked for happiness anywhere and everywhere, and in the end I realized that God hadn't abandoned me and that He would help me to return the love people gave me and to distinguish between the things that really matter and those that don't. If I can do anything for you, I will.

SHIRLEY   I want to have a child.

PAUL   Seriously? With that Italian guy? What's his name . . .
Angelo?

SHIRLEY (*Somberly*)   Renato.

PAUL   A rising young actor . . .

SHIRLEY   You're well informed.

PAUL   You see, I haven't forgotten you. I read what they write
about you. I know the papers like a scandal and often write
any old thing, but at least it gave me pleasure to see your
career going so well.

SHIRLEY   My best friend rang me yesterday evening. She told
me that, since I've been away, Renato has been flaunting
himself around all the nightclubs of L.A. with a twenty-
year-old blonde, the daughter of my producer.

PAUL   I'm so sorry . . . Do you really love him, this Renato?

SHIRLEY   Let's just say he's an antidote to the passage of time
. . . But I think I'm more obsessed with my own lost youth
than with him . . . Of course, he loves me. He likes to run
around when I'm not there, but as soon as I return he'll be
begging me to take him back.

PAUL (*Skeptical, but not discouraging*)   If you're sure . . . I
guess everything will sort itself out . . .

SHIRLEY   No.

PAUL (*Weary, and somewhat abashed*)   Listen, in the end, it's
your business. I can talk it over with you if you think it will
help, but I think you're the only one who can decide if it's
the right thing for you. You've decided to break up with
Renato in order to have a more serious relationship with
someone else, is that it?

SHIRLEY   Yes.

PAUL   Well, then . . . If you have really decided to start a family, I'm sure you'll find the right man, a man who knows how to love you and can make you happy.

SHIRLEY   And I'm sure I won't.

PAUL   Why?

SHIRLEY   Because I know him and he's already taken.

PAUL   Are you sure you love him? Are you sure he's the right one?

SHIRLEY (*Passionately*)   Yes. Oh, yes, I'm sure. But it may be too late.

PAUL   If you're really sure, you should take a chance. You don't find true love too often in life. What were you doing with Renato, if you love another man? You shouldn't waste your feelings. Have you been running away from love like this for a long time?

SHIRLEY (*In a whisper*)   Yes.

PAUL   Do you think this man loves you?

SHIRLEY   I don't know. (*She lowers her eyes.*)   Do you still love me?

Paul looks at her; then, after a pause, gently:

PAUL   Shirley, were you talking about me?

SHIRLEY (*Emotionally*)   You're the one I love.

Paul walks to the window and looks out, not speaking. Shirley goes to the mirror, cleans up her face, fixes her hair. She fills her glass and goes over to Paul, still standing with his back to her. She places her hand on his shoulder. He turns round; she gives him the glass. He turns back to the window and drinks.

SHIRLEY (*Calmly*)   I'm not asking you to come and live with me; I know that's not possible. I just want you to give me a baby.

PAUL (*Turning to face her*)   You're crazy! Why me?

SHIRLEY   Give me a child and I won't ask anything more of you. You'll never hear from me again.

PAUL   Shirley, try to understand. That's not the way to have children. A child has a right to know its father.

SHIRLEY   I'll say you're dead.

PAUL   Very nice. I can see you've thought of everything. Do you realize what it is you're saying? I can't believe you're serious.

Shirley moves away, slumps down onto the couch and starts to cry.

SHIRLEY (*In tears*)   I was sure, I was sure . . .

Paul comes over to her and raises her head, angrily.

PAUL   Stop that. You're an excellent actress, you know how to turn on the tears, but we're not in a movie now. So enough of the melodrama, OK?

SHIRLEY (*Crying even harder*)   Leave me alone, I beg you, leave me alone . . .

Paul sinks into an armchair.

Shirley comes over to him and falls at his feet.

SHIRLEY   Forgive me.

Still kneeling next to the armchair, Shirley lays her head in Paul's lap.

SHIRLEY (*In a whisper*)   Give me a baby, Paul.

She lowers the shoulders of her dress, accentuating her décolletage.

SHIRLEY   Do I still please you?

Paul drags Shirley to the couch. They kiss. He strokes her legs . . .

SHIRLEY (*Triumphant*)   You'll see, it's *you* I'll launch in Hollywood. I'll do everything to make sure you become famous and Renato stays a nobody. He'll see that he can't get away with making a fool out of Shirley. (*More controlled:*)   Come . . . we will be happy . . .

Paul leaps to his feet.

PAUL   So that's it! That's what you wanted—to take me back in your luggage to make your boy toy angry . . .

SHIRLEY   No . . . No, that's not true! It's for you, Paul, for us! Come with me, you won't regret it!

PAUL   You're not thinking of anyone but yourself. Yourself and your own pleasure. As usual. People are just like puppets to you. But you don't have as many strings as you used to to manipulate men. Now if you'll excuse me, I'm expected at home.

He heads for the door.

SHIRLEY   You're being unfair, so unfair!

She starts to cry again.

SHIRLEY   Then go. I don't ever want to see you again.

He leaves. Shirley stops crying immediately and picks up the phone.

SHIRLEY   Hello . . . Could you put me through to my PA, please . . . Hello, Babe. Would you be so good as to look up a number for me, name of Bobby Wesson . . . Yes, that's it, the car salesman. *With a cute smile and a devilish glint in his eye.* No problem, he'll remember me . . .

τ

*I*f I were Babe, thought Carmen as she watched the TV absently, I'd prefer a male. Her Bobby's not bad, he's quite willing, but she'll never get what she wants from him. Men are ill-conceived, corrupted from the start. If only they could be reeducated. Today women are organized and well-informed, but although they are capable of significant action, they are still very limited.

Firstly, men don't understand half of what they're told. They don't actually listen. You wouldn't think we speak the same language. They really are alien beings. I've hung out with them since I don't know when, and even I think I'll never understand them completely. Women like to kid themselves that men are, so to speak, crudely made, basically very simple, and as long as you hold them by the right end you can do whatever you like with them. Lots of men think like that too. The truth is, there's nothing on earth more complex or sadder than a man.

The truth is that / I have mud on my hands / from digging for weeds. / The truth is that / I bring them to you. / It's true that / I work to find them / and I complain / as I dig and pull. / The truth is that / when I come back here / and I see your face / I don't mind / this work anymore.

It's a poem by the Cree Indians that I discovered on the Net, my spiritual home. Nature, sure, Nature. But Silicon Valley is part of Nature.

Mud on my hands: that's men, that's their sadness. Men are born lost, so they fight, drink, lose it, take drugs, they are obsessed with sex, power, money, glory, whatever, anything that lets them forget themselves, they flagellate one another and themselves, they'd rather die but are too full of life, men's strength and energy are much greater than women's, but so is their vanity, and their despair.

I'd put him on all fours on the living room table, legs slightly apart, buttocks turned toward the door, so that when I came in I'd immediately see his taut ass, his balls and cock dangling between his legs. He'd be completely at my disposal, I'd do whatever I liked with him, he'd never ask me for anything I didn't want to do, I'd never have to fend off his advances or give in to them, he would be neither jealous nor proud nor repressed, he'd refuse none of my fantasies. He wouldn't look at other women, I would reign supreme and he would not regret it for a moment. I'd spend hours dressing him and undressing him, cleaning him, washing him down below, a long wash down below, he'd have a collection of uniforms, one day a fireman, the next a legionnaire, or a policeman, or a general . . . Whenever I liked I would open his fly and slide my hand in, or between the buttons of his shirt, under his T-shirt or down the back of his pants. I'd fill his penis with strawberry yogurt, or lemon, or plain, nothing too heavy or sickly, and I would decide when it would go off in my mouth. Or else I'd use warm water or a gentle, perfumed gel and shower myself anywhere I wanted to. He would be able to make love to me for as long and as often as I required, until my desire was exhausted. I could amuse myself by masturbating him and sucking him in every possible position, and even when I was asleep I could keep him inside my vagina, or my ass, or my mouth, or in my hand without him ever getting sick of it. He'd become erect or limp on command like a real man, only more reliable. His face and tongue would become ultrasophisticated vibrators whenever I wanted, and as he would be extremely supple, a contortionist, even, I could, for example, sit him on the floor, with his head leaning back over a chair, start him up and sit on him as I ate or watched TV. When I wanted to punish him for being an insatiable pig, I'd give him a good spanking, I'd make him lie on the floor at the foot of my bed or out on the veranda, stark naked, in midwinter, so that Shirley Gordon could see how I treat men, or else I'd dress him as a woman, make him wear high heels, stockings, a bra, tiny panties that his large genitals spilled out of, makeup and jewelry, and I'd sodomize him with the most ridiculous objects, in the most humiliating positions, I'd piss on him, I'd stick things in his mouth, I'd cover his body with whipped cream which I'd lick off him, I'd smear him with honey and leave him out for the bees, I'd organize parties, and when everyone was drunk I'd give him to my guests to amuse themselves with, I'd lock him in the closet, I'd tell him horrible things, I'd spit on him, I'd shoot him a glare, I'd threaten him, I'd make fun of him, I'd lay him on the ground and walk all over him as if he weren't there . . . And when I'd had enough of abusing him, when I felt sorry for him, I'd console him, I'd whisper to him, I'd give him my breasts to suck, I'd stroke him, I'd kiss him all over and ask his forgiveness, I'd promise to do everything he wanted, I'd tell him he's handsome, that he gives me the most incredible orgasms, that I like seeing him come, that he can fuck me all over, I'd spoil him to death, I'd let him taste all my orifices, I'd make him spurt his yogurt out over the whole house, I'd tell him I'd never had such pleasure, and what's more, it would be true.

At night I'd sleep in his arms, he'd hold me tight to him, I'd rest my head against his powerful chest, I'd hold his penis in my hand so as not to fall into a pit of nightmares, he'd be there, always, my teddy bear, my wolf, my angel, my demon, my infallible phallus, my knot, my rope, stretching down into the void, the well, from my throat to my sex, my spinal cord, my horse, my game, my prey, my colossus, my god, my fear, my pain, my death, I'd raise an altar in the house dedicated to his body, and that house would be me, my soul, which I'd give to him.

υ

he slut!" Babe exclaimed, totally infuriated.

"That's dumb," Carmen observed. "Why did she try to resurrect things with her ex rather than just go out there and find herself a new one?"

"'Just' . . . That's easy to say . . . Men always make out they're up for anything, but when it comes to the crunch . . ."

"I see . . . If I'm catching your drift, I could have a long wait before you bring one home for me."

"Don't be angry, my darling . . . You'll have one tomorrow, I swear."

"Yeah, whatever. I've had enough of this house. No one pays any attention to me. This afternoon I was left locked up here all alone. You'd think I didn't even exist. It's a good thing Shirley came to visit . . ."

"Shirley Gordon? Did you let her in?"

129

"We had a bit of a chat . . . She's so sexy! And very refined . . . She even read me a poem . . ."

"You're playing with me, you little tease . . ."

"No I'm not. It was a Chippewa poem about a storm
breaking: *From one half / of the sky / comes the sound / of he who
lives there.* It's better than what you make me watch on TV,
don't you think? Look, there she is again!"

Babe heard the front door open and gave a start. She was
stretched out on the ethnic throw on the couch, her head resting on the pillow of Carmen's cool white thighs.

"Honey, are you home?" came Bobby's voice.

A little later she heard him shout from the garage, but
couldn't make out what he was asking for. Elvis was singing
as if on a vinyl record, "*Are you lonesome tonight?*" Bobby came
upstairs and repeated his question from the stairwell:

"Where's the axe?"

"I lent it to Shirley Gordon," Babe replied.

"*I wonder if,*" Elvis continued, his voice from beyond the
grave chewing up the words into an overly slow, sickly sweet
rap, "*you're lonesome tonight.*"

"You need the axe?" asked Babe as she removed the de-
frosted pizza from the microwave.

"I've added some cheese and some oil," she added, clearly
pleased with the result.

And with her thick-padded oven glove she held aloft the
Indefinable Golden Puffball, pumped up like a tire, dazzling
as a flashgun, resplendent in its majestic and holy splendor.

"Hmmm!" said Bobby, licking his lips. "That looks
pretty tasty . . . !"

"Don't it just? I wonder what she wanted the axe for . . ."

"She didn't tell you?"

"Oh, who knows with that one . . . Did you need it?"

"No. Who'd have thought you could get so much melted cheese on top of a pizza! I hope it doesn't clog up our guts!"

"Oh, Bobby! That's disgusting! Do you think I did wrong to lend her the axe?"

"No, why?"

"Dunno . . . You don't think there's a bit of a resemblance to Jack Nicholson?"

"Huh? The pizza?"

"Shirley Gordon."

"Ah! Ooh! Yeah! Maybe . . . I don't know, I'd need to take a closer look . . . Hmm, really fine . . ."

"Shirley Gordon?"

"The pizza."

"What do you mean, you'd need to take a closer look? We've lived next door to her for ten years and you don't know what she looks like?"

"Yeah, 'course I do . . . It's just I've never noticed a resemblance to Marilyn Manson . . ."

"I didn't say Marilyn Manson, I said Jack Nicholson. Jack Nicholson in *The Shining*."

"Hey, now you mention it . . . Maybe you shouldn't have lent her the axe, honey."

"Excuse me, but I don't find that funny. That woman is nuts—you know as well as I do. Please listen to me. What I'm trying to tell you is that it'll end badly . . ."

"What are you talking about?"

"What am I talking about? You ask me what I'm talking about? Take a look at the world around you . . ."

"You know, Marilyn Manson's not bad either . . ."

"I'm sure she's planning something nasty for us. She's always spying on us . . ."

"Don't get carried away. She's just a poor girl who's got nothing to do all day, that's all."

"'Girl'? That big, flabby pudding? Oh, you make me sick."

"Hey, it's nothing to do with me."

"OK, OK. You let her come on to you like she's Miss Universe herself, but it's nothing to do with you . . . Meanwhile, she's always there. You wouldn't believe me if I told you . . ."

"What's with you this evening? Have you had a lousy day or something? Has Shirley upset you?"

"Will you please not call her Shirley!"

"What do you want me to call her? Jack Nicholson?"

"Shirley Gordon. Shirley Gordon is not our friend. I would like you to remember that."

"I don't give a damn about Shirley Gordon, OK?"

"OK."

"OK."

"*I*t's just a pity . . ."

"What?"

"We were doing fine, Carmen, you and me . . ."

". . ."

"Babe?"

"Yes?"

"You asleep?"

"No."

"Do we have to have Carmen lying between us?"

"Why?"

"I want you . . ."

"Take her, her . . ."

"Again?"

"She wants to."

"What about you? Don't you want to?"

"She's insatiable."

"A threesome, then . . ."

"No, her. I'll guide you, I know what she wants.

"And me? Do you know what I want?"

"She knows. Come on, do what I tell you . . ."

S weet Jesus!" Babe gasped as she saw the patch of blood spreading over Jimmy's white T-shirt. "Sweet Jesus, what happened to you?"

Before she had opened the door all she could see was his chubby, boyish face through the spyhole. He looked the same as usual. How could she have guessed the state he was in? And now he was just standing there on the doorstep, the axe in his hand, bleeding from his side, looking as if nothing were amiss.

"It's nothing, ma'am," he replied. "It's the axe. It's heavy . . . Mom asked me to bring your axe back and I fell . . ."

"You fell? What do you mean, you fell? Where did you fall?

"On the steps," he said, turning around to point at the white wooden steps to the veranda, now stained with blood.

My God, thought Babe. I've got to take care of this boy.

They stood there in the doorway—Jimmy with his head lowered, his cheeks red, one arm dangling, the other stretched by the weight of the axe, the blade of which was grazing his ankle; Babe leaning slightly forward, her arms wide, as if she were about to take hold of a big baby that some teenage girl had abandoned on her porch—and like freshly caught fish they gasped for breath, their mouths wide-open.

Babe suddenly realized she had lost the cord of her plum-colored robe (still unwashed) and that it was flapping open over her naked body, revealing a rectangular gash of flesh from her neck to her fake blonde pubic hair.

The house was as silent as a bell jar, a giant napoleon; they had to pass through a vast mille-feuille of windows, Babe leading, Jimmy following, and their ears, their heads were filled with the sound of shattering glass as they walked through to the living room, a tinkling cacophony in the desert.

Carmen lay stretched out on her back on the couch. She was wearing the furry G-string from Pearl's, with the matching bra and garter belt and sheer black stockings, which crinkled round her ankles.

The woman started speaking and the words flew out of her mouth like clouds of birds and skimmed over Jimmy's body, pecking at it. He stood in front of Carmen, and when Mrs. Wesson came back from the bathroom with the jar of antiseptic, and when she stood right beside him and asked him to take off his T-shirt, he dropped the axe and reached out toward her. He could just touch her breast with the tips of his fingers. And they undressed in a sort of slow, disorderly way that at the same time was a mad rush, and there was nothing hard about Jimmy's fat, white, warm, moist young body, nothing except his erect penis, and there was nothing hard in Babe's

136

gentle curves, nothing except her dark eyes, and there was nothing red in all this flesh, nothing except the blood that flowed from Jimmy's wound and from Babe's sex, which she displayed to Jimmy, legs apart, knees bent, opening it with both hands, just to show him what was what. And when they were completely naked, they pulled aside the living room table, laid Carmen on the floor, and Jimmy had to lie on top of her and do it, with the woman's hand guiding him inside, That was my first woman, Jimmy will think later, and he will not be entirely sure whether it is Babe or Carmen he is thinking about, afterward there was blood on Carmen's skin, they all had blood and sperm on their skin, Mrs. Wesson asked Jimmy to do a whole load of stuff, and Jimmy wanted to do everything she asked just so long as they touched his dick and pushed it into tight, warm, damp places, where he found paradise, from which he never wanted to be banished.

"*J*iiimmy! Yoo-hoo, Jimmy! Answer me, dear, it's your mom!"

Shirley's mules clicked on the wooden steps, then she started rapping on the door with her fat little hand.

"Babe? Are you there? What's my Jimmy up to? Jiiimmy! You're not stuffing your face with cakes, are you? Come home, and stop annoying Mrs. Wesson! . . . Babe? You there, Babe? I sent Jimmy round with your axe, and . . ."

"Yeah, yeah, I'm coming!" Jimmy grunted, pushing away Babe, who was trying to help him get dressed.

"Sweet Jesus, you scared me! I thought something had happened to you with that axe! The steps are covered with blood. Is Mrs. Wesson there with you?"

137

"I'm here, Shirley! Jimmy and I were just having a little chat . . ."

Wrapped up in her stained robe, Babe appeared in the doorway, determined not to let anyone inside the house.

"Come on, Jimmy," she called out, giving Shirley a firm stare that said "Keep your distance." "Hurry up, your mom's waiting for you!"

The boy's chubby face appeared over her shoulder, and she stepped aside to let him pass. At the sight of her son's bloody T-shirt, Shirley started screaming, the familiar piercing screams she used to express both horror and joy. (Consequently, the neighborhood found these grotesque manifestations of her existence completely unfathomable.)

Babe quickly shut the door. Then she went skipping and humming, like a child on her way home from school, to the kitchen, where she opened the refrigerator door and knelt there in ecstasy before the light.

Her arms full of desserts, she came back to the living room and turned on the TV.

χ

The ground is covered with straw, some sort of hay, the enclosure surrounded by walls, not very high, to allow the natural light in, and it is quiet here, there is nothing else to do but to remain suspended in time like dust on the savannah, people can look in through the wide grille of the gate, the iron bars are thick, black and widely spaced, though not so wide that a child could squeeze through. In a corner at the back can be made out a sort of niche, a human-size niche. Babe is there somewhere, from time to time she may move a little, and from time to time she is spotted or even observed for a while, but she is not the most popular animal in the zoo, her enclosure is quite modest, one could walk by it without even noticing it, and it is tucked away in a quiet corner of the park, there are never many people in front of the bars, they glance in as they walk past and don't see anything, but they aren't too disappointed,

139

because they weren't expecting to see anything interesting, there was a time when they flocked in to see the human beings in the zoo, but now . . .

"I had a weird dream," said Babe.

"Last night?" asked Bobby.

"No, no. Just now."

"You dream while you're awake?"

"Maybe it wasn't a dream."

"The whisky, then . . ."

"Do you think so?"

"Dunno. It makes me think odd thoughts . . ."

"Really? Maybe we should drink more often."

"Take it easy, baby. I don't want to make love to a drunk."

"Really?"

"If baby wants a feed, have some of this instead . . ."

They were sitting at the kitchen table.

"Do you know what I think?" Babe said. "Only the stars have the right to feed us. They never stop feeding us light, even during the day when we can't see them, and afterward, we have nothing left . . ."

Bobby looked at the almost empty bottle.

"I'll give you your goddamn light," he muttered.

"It was the olives that gave me the idea. I looked in the refrigerator and I saw the olives. That made me think about whisky. So I said to myself, Hey, why don't I have a little drink while I'm waiting for Bobby."

"And what does my dick make you think about?"

"Carmen."

"Oh, can't you forget about her for a moment . . ."

"The poor thing, I left her on the floor in the living room . . ."

"Screw Carmen . . ."

"Oh, Bobby!"

"What? Huh? Aren't we OK, just the two of us?"

"All I have to say is, if you carry on having hard-ons like that, I'll cut it off!"

"Oh yeah? And how you going to have your fun when you've done that?"

"You think I need that to have fun? I DON'T NEED THAT!"

"I can see you don't need it. You prefer women!"

"I DON'T PREFER WOMEN! I prefer Carmen, that's all!"

"OK, I get it, loud and clear. So go and have a drink with her, instead of leaving her lying on the floor of the living room. Go on, go talk to her! She's a great conversationalist!"

"Is that why you brought her into our house? Because of her conversation?"

"I got her because you didn't want to fuck anymore."

"Sure I wanted to fuck. Once a week. That's enough, isn't it?"

"That's enough for you, but not for me. A man has his needs . . ."

"I see . . . Men have 'needs,' like they need to go to the bathroom . . ."

"Yeah, right, and women, too. They do it like they're constipated. With an effort, when they can't avoid it anymore."

"Is this about me?"

"No, it's not about you."

"Who then?"

"Nobody."

"In any case, I don't have a body anymore. You don't have a body anymore. There aren't any bodies, just the memory of bodies."

"That's enough . . ."

"We are slowly disappearing."

"Babe, put the bottle down. Come here. Let's just go to bed and sleep together."

"It's too late."

"Come on, honey, I love you."

"She'll kill us, and we won't even be able to rest in peace."

"Come on, honey. Let's go to bed. We don't need to make love to prove we're still lovers. Why are you crying?"

"For us . . . For Jimmy . . ."

"Jimmy? Shirley's son?"

"Don't call her Shirley!"

"Oh, give it a rest . . . 'The neighbor,' if you prefer."

"'Shirley Gordon.'"

"What about her, anyway? Has something happened to her son?"

"He's lost his body."

"What do you mean? Has he had an accident?"

"It was a sacrifice. Shirley Gordon sent her own son to be sacrificed. I'm scared, Bobby! We're all destined! I know who Shirley Gordon is!"

"Of course you do . . ."

"She's the one who sent Carmen to us."

"No she isn't . . ."

"She is God. Shirley Gordon is God incarnate. I'm scared . . ."

ight fell like a skyscraper, col-
lapsing on top of the living with the inhuman force of the dark.
Carmen lay on the floor in the lounge, her stomach stained
with blood.

"We can't keep her," said Bobby.

"No," said Babe.

Together they lifted her up and laid her on the ethnic
throw on the couch. Babe freshened her up while Bobby went
to find her some clothes in the bedroom. He chose the black
outfit that Babe had bought for her parents' funeral: they had
died in a crash, far away from America, on their first-ever trip
abroad.

In her mourning clothes, Carmen looked more alive than
ever. Babe cried silently, her eyes hollowed out, her features
drawn, her face aged by anguish, as she prepared her lover with
tenderness and respect. Bobby sat in a chair, watching them

with his strange, unseeing gaze, which for once seemed more frightened than unsettling.

Babe tried out several pairs of shoes on Carmen, then decided to leave her barefoot. She realized that this decision gave her a deep satisfaction and sense of consolation. As if, despite everything, she was preserving Carmen's true nature: wild at heart.

When Babe had done Carmen's hair and makeup (after a number of attempts, for her hands were trembling), they carried her down to the cellar. They had to stop several times on the stairs: her body felt like it was full of lead, and her dead weight pulled on their arms like cold molasses, opaque and dark like her staring eyes.

They installed her in the back of the Cadillac and fastened her in with loving care, as if the better to hide from her the fact that they had decided to dump her by the side of the road somewhere. Bobby sat in the driver's seat with a sense of ceremony: it was a car for special occasions. Babe sat next to him, yanked her robe down over her knees, fastened her seat belt and stared straight ahead with a dignified air.

The limousine glided majestically up the garage ramp, the headlights turned off so as not to attract attention from the neighbors, pale in the night like a gigantic pink dung beetle emerging from its hole at the hour when the ubiquitous, bright, shiny creatures of the daytime are going off to sleep.

At the end of the alley, on the other side of the crossroads, was parked a large 4×4. It began signaling with its dazzling lights. Bobby decided to switch on the lights of the Cadillac. As they turned left, they passed in front of the 4×4. Inside was Shirley Gordon. Her eyes shone like a cat's; her fingers, with their painted nails, were wrapped round the steering wheel like a spider's legs. She seemed to smile, raised her right hand and gave a little wave, wiggling her fingers as if they were attached to invisible strings, as if the dark in which the light patches of her face and hands floated was hiding an army of puppets whose dance she was controlling. Bobby put his foot down on the accelerator.

There was no one behind them except her. She had followed them across the housing project, followed them onto the highway, into the flux of fleeing headlights, and, when in a vain attempt to shake her off Bobby had turned into a side road, so quickly that his tires screeched around the hairpin, she had kept the same distance, as if she were happy to be dragged along by them, as if she had them in the stranglehold of her dark lasso in the dark night, and as if no swerve or kick or sudden change of course would cause her to loosen her grip.

And now Bobby was driving down this straight, deserted side road, bordered by a dark forest. Shirley Gordon, driving behind them, was blinding him with her headlights. Next to him, his wife Babe was asking him to go back. He could vaguely hear her saying that she didn't really want to abandon Carmen, or else they could do it another time, it was better just to go quietly home now, he could feel the panic rising from their bodies and filling the enclosed space of the vehicle so palpably that it felt like concrete being poured round them and solidifying, preventing them from changing course or abandoning their goal, obliging them to drive ever onward.

He had lost all notion of time when the splendid Cadillac spun out of control, lost its grip on the road and flew off a bend into the dark mass of the forest, where it embedded itself in a din of screams and twisted metal.

* * *

The day was dry and clear. Tommy and Carroll, in the first of a short line of cars, stopped in front of the window of the drive-in funeral parlor, where the attendant passed them the two urns. They took one each and placed them on their knees, while the pastor, wired up with a microphone, came over and began reciting a standard homage to the deceased, whose names, Babe and Bobby, he read off a form that he had pulled from inside his toga. He concluded the ceremony with an absurdly theatrical prayer, in imitation of the style of the wealthiest TV evangelist of the time.

Carroll placed the urns beneath her legs, and they set off slowly, followed by five other cars. A large 4×4 brought up the rear. The pastor's gaze lingered on the woman who was driving it, a dark, corpulent woman who was giving him flirtatious looks. Next to her was a pretty girl in a black outfit, staring fixedly ahead, sitting upright and motionless next to the chubby boy with whom she shared the seat. Before the vehicle drove away and disappeared round the bend, Shirley Gordon, face painted like a tart's, popped her head out of the window and whispered:

"Hi, Reverend!"

What a slut! the minister couldn't help thinking, as he felt a surge of sexual arousal insinuate itself into his body like a serpent and spit out a desire for death.

ω

hen the bodies of Babe Smith
and Bobby Wesson slid into the furnace of the World Village
crematorium, the infernal heat that raged around their coffins
expelled the torpors of death and ignited searing dreams, the
ultimate fantasies of their dismal existences.

Bobby, who had fantasized all his life about the array of
girls with sculpted bodies who posed with their legs apart in
men's magazines, or who indulged in every imaginable prac-
tice in repetitive videos, their charms silicone-enhanced for the
voyeuristic pleasure of contemporary manhood, Bobby, who,
though he had had his fair share of dogs, had only ever considered that the most attractive girls met his rigid criteria (as
vigorous as those of the social body as a whole), Bobby, then,
in a flashing contraction-dilation of time, succumbed one last
time to earthly pleasures thanks to his fat, vulgar, no-spring-
chicken neighbor, Shirley Gordon.

The scene of his cremation dream was identical in every detail to the residential zone where he and Babe had bought the house of their dreams a few years earlier. So much so that one might think it was purely the flames of death that had inspired this illusion. For the fantasy that sputtered forth from his corpse that day was perhaps no more than an old lucubration, forged in the course of the never-ending rosary of nights when he was driven, in order to palliate his conjugal frustration, to indulge in secret onanism, the ardent fist, subsequently to rejoin his tender but cold other half in sleep.

Be that as it may, the furnace, which had witnessed many such scenes, observed, with professional indifference, this final spectacle produced by the incineration of a body that had once been alive, young and handsome, and full of the usual disgusting desires of the human species. From the heart of the flames, spurting from Bobby's liver, two wide-open eyes appeared, glistening in a halo of half-light.

From this static shot a swift zoom-out, revealing in succession Bobby's head, motionless, lying on a pink pillow; then the comforter, beneath which could be made out two elongated forms; then the whole bed, the bedroom; and while the lens, which was probably trained on this scene through the window, continued its backward flight, the night grew darker and shadows attached themselves to the outside walls like leprous sores, and when the whole of the Wesson house could finally be seen in the frame, it seemed so ghostly, sinister and ruined that one might have expected the dream to stop right there and then.

But the mysterious camera continued to roll, and there was Bobby in his pajamas, outside on the doorstep, watching the following: a line of men, all similarly dressed in striped pajamas, illuminated by the yellow light of a sliver of moon intermittently masked by scudding clouds, stretching from the house next door, down the street and ending who knows where in the pitch-black night.

The front door of the Gordon house was open, the only clear rectangle of light in the whole scene. Old Stanley, Shirley's husband, stood in the doorway in a suit and tie, ushering the men in, one by one and two per minute. Bobby walked across the lawn with great difficulty—for every step demanded a considerable effort of his benumbed body, and the effect produced was one of ponderous slow motion.

When he finally reached his neighbors' property, a murmur went up and traveled the length of the line: "Join the line! Join the line like everyone else!" The men's faces, perched like scarecrow heads on top of the stripy outfits, which seemed to hang from coat hangers rather than bodies, grew longer and filled with ever more alarming shadows as their disgruntlement turned to anger, then to hatred. No one moved a muscle—each man was firmly rooted to his place in the line, which he had no intention of surrendering—but the line as a whole quivered like the spume on the crest of a wave which was about to break over the miserable human body that had ventured out to face the sea. Bobby took a step back and turned his head to catch Stanley's eye—old, skinny, taciturn Stanley, with whom he had never exchanged more than a dozen words at a time, and who now seemed to be his only means of escaping from this nightmare. With a slow, broad sweep of his arm, Stanley waved him over.

Bobby cast a glance at the line. There was a murmur of disapproval at the doorman's action, but they soon grew resigned and settled down. He reached Stan in a few strides, and was placed at the front of the line. A few seconds later, he was let in.

Once he was through the door he realized that the line continued inside the house, stretching upstairs, one man on each step. A strong, feral smell impregnated the hallway and became more powerful between the narrow walls of the stairwell. On reaching the bottom step, each man drew his penis out of the fly of his pants and started to masturbate. The line kept its shape but stirred with light moans and groans and small spasmodic movements, caused either by the stimulation of members or by the protests of those who felt encroached upon by the fellow behind in this atmosphere of enforced promiscuity.

Every thirty seconds, the line collectively took a step up. Bobby soon arrived at the bottom step, whereupon he swiftly did as was required, because, firstly, there was little chance he would be able to go back, and secondly, although disgusted by his situation, he was unable to resist the enormous sexual tension that pervaded this narrow passage and he was already erect. Like the others, he grabbed his penis, which had virtually popped out of his pajamas of its own accord, and began to stroke it slowly, taking care to delay his pleasure until the unknown but inexorable end. Among the faces grimacing with excitement that he saw in profile at the turn of the stairs, he recognized several of his neighbors, but, other than feverishly working away to maintain their erections, they all behaved as normally as if they were standing in line at the supermarket or in a social security office.

The smell of this collective rut became more powerful the higher Bobby climbed the stairs. After about ten minutes he arrived at the top. The line, still in the same rhythm, shuffled into a bedroom.

When he reached the door, Bobby finally discovered what was awaiting him. Lying on her back in the center of her double bed, her legs spread wide and raised up as if for an induced birth, Shirley offered a choice of orifice to the men who took their turns with her every thirty seconds.

Even more than usual, her face was caked in makeup. She wore a totally see-through tiny pink baby-doll nightie, which displayed all her fat white flesh; her stomach was trussed like a sausage in a garter belt that held a pair of sheer black stockings halfway up her thighs. The slip had been ripped to allow access to her breasts; her face was smeared with red lipstick and black and blue eye shadow. From her thighs up to her hair, her body was splashed with sperm. She didn't move, but merely emitted a cluck of satisfaction each time a man penetrated her and ejaculated somewhere in or over her.

When his turn came, after a moment's hesitation, Bobby chose her mouth. He crouched over Shirley's face, pushed his penis in and after three thrusts came in long convulsive spurts. Half suffocated, Shirley clucked through her nose, looking him in the face with an even more depraved expression than usual.

He couldn't have held out a second longer. Liberated, he began to laugh nervously, and withdrew to make way for the next man. That was when he realized with horror that it was his turn to be transformed instantaneously into ashes, like all those who had preceded him and whose dust now littered the floor in a thick, warm layer.

Thus was the body and soul of Bobby Wesson extinguished forever. As for Babe Smith, his deceased wife, she experienced in the furnace a final surge of life and a much simpler dream, though in its way no less delicious and terrifying. She could feel a warm, ample, fleshy appendage push itself so fully and forcefully into her mouth that it yanked her, perhaps for all time, from her eternal sleep. This flesh was both a giant breast and a giant penis, at once delectable and suffocating. Shifting between terror and greed, Babe kept her eyes closed, and in the dark fury of her incineration continued to suck, with growing appetite.